# *Her Reluctant Cowboy*

## SILVER CREEK RANCH
### BOOK THIRTEEN

## DARIE MCCOY

ISBN Ebook: 978-1-961999-25-1

Paperback: 978-1-961999-26-8

Cover design: EmCat Designs

Proofreading: Phoenix Pen

# Content Advisory

Please note that this book is intended for mature audiences. It contains material some may find disturbing or uncomfortable. The FMC, Vivienne, is an army veteran who has experienced trauma during her time in the service, causing PTSI (Post-Traumatic Stress Injury). There are mentions of her trauma and triggers. If PTSI is something you find disturbing, I understand if you forgo this read.

This book also contains adult situations, language, and graphic sexual interactions.

# The Silver Creek Ranch

Forgotten military heroes who needed a helping hand re-entering the society they had been sworn to protect. The Silver Creek Ranch provided a space where these cowboys could work the land and get back in touch with the men they once were.

The battles of war left scars on each of them.

Healing was what these cowboys needed.

Who knew it would comprise the touch, kiss, and love of a good woman?

*The Silver Creek Ranch is an interracial cowboy romance shared world. Each captivating story is filled with plenty of heat and will leave your heart racing with the desire to devour every one of them.*

# Her Reluctant Cowboy

***Old Wounds. New beginnings. One unexpected chance to get it right.***

Four years out of the army, Vivienne Daley finds something which brought her peace. Working with the horses at the Silver Creek Ranch. It's just her and the sweet beasts who need her TLC. And, as far as she's concerned that's all she needs. Going home to Lone Star Ridge isn't in her plans, until the future of the Daley family ranch is on the line, and she has to seek aid from the one man she's avoided for years.

Rhinehart Stephens has spent the majority of his adulthood ranch-life adjacent, but not actually participating. He'd even given up his share of the Stephens family ranch to his brother to pursue a career in business. However, no amount of distancing himself from ranch life could keep him away when Vivienne Daley returns to Lone Star Ridge and asks for his help.

Her desire to save the Daley ranch will take more than Vivienne can do alone. But losing the ranch isn't the only thing at risk with Rhinehart Stephens involved. Can they put their past behind them and work together?  Or, will their history cause her reluctant cowboy to turn his back on their future?

*For KWB, I hope you know the way you helped me be better every time my fingers hit the keyboard. Love you to the moon and back.*

"There is nothing so easy but that it becomes difficult when you do it with reluctance,"

— TERENCE (PUBLIUS TERENTIUS AFER)

# Prologue

"YOU'RE GONNA DO WHAT?"

Dropping her feet to the floor, Vivienne sat upright at her tiny desk, staring incredulously at her granny's face on the cellphone screen. Her grandma raised a single eyebrow. With her chin resting on her hand, she stared back at Vivienne.

"I said I'm gonna sell the ranch. I'm keeping the house, but I don't need all this land, and I'm not interested in running these cows anymore."

Staring at her granny like she'd grown a second head, Vivienne tried to wrap her mind around what she'd just heard. Since when had her granny run the cows anyway? Probably decades ago, long before Grandpa Jessie passed away. Hell, probably while Vivienne's dad was still in diapers.

Okay, maybe not that long; her dad was sixty-four.

"Granny, you haven't been on a horse to run cows since before I was born."

"How would you know? You weren't born yet."

Grandma Hattie Mae was the first person to encourage Vivienne's love of horses to begin with. To hear her say she was selling the ranch was like taking a hot shoeing iron and shoving it into Vivienne's chest. Ignoring her granny's snappy comeback, Vivienne tried a different tactic.

"Granny, you can't sell the ranch. It's been in the Daley family almost since Reconstruction."

"I beg your pardon? My name is on the deed to this place. I can do what I want with my property. Besides, none of you kids are interested in working cattle anymore. Your daddy and his brothers have their company. We don't need this place to secure our family's future like we did in the past."

Running her gaze over the slightly worn carpet in the little room she'd converted into a makeshift office at the Silver Creek Ranch, Vivienne's heart plummeted as her mind raced, trying to figure out what she could do to stop her grandmother from making a colossal mistake.

Mentally, she went through possible solutions to keep the land in family hands. Why had no one told her about this? She'd talked to Autumn not two days ago, and nothing about this had come up. When her cousin moved in with Rothschild Stephens at the Lazy Creek, Vivienne thought it would mean she'd get more first-hand information on Grandma Hattie's health and overall well-being.

What was the point of Autumn living next door and not knowing what was happening? Vivienne pushed aside the distance between the ranches due to the size of each spread. Autumn was right next door!

"Granny, what if we found someone to completely take care of the cattle side of things? What about Herb or Clay? Herb has been with you for almost two decades. Surely he has the experience to fully take over operations. Or what about Clay? Hasn't he taken on more responsibility? He could help Herb."

"Don't you think I've considered what would happen to the boys? I've been leaning on Herb for years now. I pay him well, but not well enough for him to buy the place. And I damn sure ain't gonna give it to him when I'm not giving it to my own grandkids—not like y'all want it anyway."

"Don't say that, Granny!" Before Vivienne could stop herself, the words came flying out. "I want it! I want the ranch."

Silence met her declaration, giving Vivienne the chance to digest what she'd just said. Enough time passed, offering her ample opportunity to retract the spontaneous announcement. She didn't.

Her pulse thundered to the rhythm of galloping horses running in her veins. With her thoughts racing almost manically, Vivienne stood in the center of her shoebox stable office, waiting for her grandmother to say something. Anything other than repeating her plan to sell a piece of the Daley family legacy.

"Vivi..."

The resignation in her granny's tone matched her facial expression. Neither inspired hope, but Vivienne held onto it with both hands.

"Vivi... you don't want to run cows any more than I do. You love horses. Isn't that the reason you've been in South Dakota for the past three years?"

Vivienne adored horses. Working with them had helped her find her way when being an Army medic had become too much, forcing her to leave the military. But the horses weren't her only reason for staying at Silver Creek Ranch.

Here was where she'd found peace. Healing for her spirit, battered by her feelings of helplessness—like she'd let her fellow service members down. When all the advanced training she'd taken didn't matter because she couldn't save the soldiers who needed her the most.

Working with the team at Silver Creek, being a part of the day-to-day operations, and tending to the horses who needed special care had given her a new purpose. Was she willing to give that up? Was saving her family's ranch from being taken over by strangers worth leaving the place she'd found solace? It was. Vivienne couldn't explain why, but it was.

"You're right, Granny. I don't want to run cows."

Her Grandma Hattie's facial expression remained unchanged. Yet, Vivienne continued.

"Maybe it's time for the Sunset Ranch to pivot from cattle. Either way, please don't sell the ranch. Give me a chance."

Soft eyes, the same deep brown as her own, stared back at Vivienne from the phone's screen. She couldn't read her grandma's expression to determine if what she'd said made an impact. After what seemed like forever, Grandma Hattie finally responded.

"I'll hold off for six months. Not a day longer. If you want this place to continue, that's how long you have to show me. So, you need to get your behind back to Texas, Little Girl."

Relief, anxiety, and anticipation battled for dominance inside Vivienne. However, she kept the emotions off her face. Instead, she smiled, nodding at her grandma.

"Yes, ma'am. I'll be there as soon as I get things wrapped up here."

"See that you are."

Issuing her directive, Grandma Hattie ended the call, leaving Vivienne with her thoughts of wrapping things up at Silver Creek and how exactly she could follow through with pivoting the Sunset Ranch from cattle to horses. She did not know *how* to make it happen, but she refused to let it go without at least trying.

# Chapter One

RHINEHART GRINNED as he watched his brother's expression darken like thunderclouds gathering over the fields. Anyone with eyes could see Roth loved Autumn to distraction. And Rhinehart hadn't seen him deny her anything she wanted. He got the feeling the streak was about to end.

"Sugar, what did I tell you about letting our mamas talk you into social club stuff?"

"But Roth, it's for a good cause."

Using a pair of tongs, Autumn selected a foil-wrapped baked potato from the bowl at the center of the table, placing it on a plate, then adding steamed broccoli before passing the plate to Roth. He passed her a plate containing a T-bone steak. Once he served himself a steak, he put the plate down in front of him on the table.

As he watched the two work together, Rhine marveled at the easy way his grumpy older brother and his fiancée took care of one another. Rhine had dinner and/or breakfast with them at least twice a month, so he'd witnessed it many times, and consistently made the same joke.

"So… what's going on? Am I being discriminated against again today?"

Rhine was sure Roth would've lit into him if Rhine's question hadn't saved Roth from further argument with Autumn about participating in another of their mothers' crazy requests from the Ladies Auxiliary. Instead of asking what Rhinehart was talking about, Roth stared at him. Positive his brother expected him to explain himself, Rhine returned the stare instead of elaborating.

As usual, Autumn breached the gap.

"Rhine, don't start tonight. Your hands work. You're family. Not a guest. You can fix your own plate."

Smiling at her, Rhinehart ignored his brother's knowing glare.

"Yeah, but I feel left out. You put Roth's veggies on his plate; then, he put your steak on your plate. But my plate is empty."

"Get your own woman. My Sugar's not fixing your food. So, get over it and quit asking."

As the youngest Stephens sibling, needling his older brother was Rhine's birthright. He considered it his sworn duty to get under Roth's skin. Under most circumstances, he and his brother shared similar personalities—one some would call gruff or rough around the edges. The only time Rhinehart was remotely playful, one of his brothers was around, and he was giving them shit.

But he knew when to knock it off. So, he stopped. For today at least. Picking up the tongs, he selected his own baked potato before helping himself to a steak and the steamed broccoli.

It didn't take long for the discussion to shift to things going on at the ranch and Autumn's job as an attorney at her family's company. Rhine listened as the two talked, without contributing much beyond the occasional question to let them know he hadn't zoned out. That was until Autumn mentioned her cousin returning to Lone Star Ridge.

If Rhine hadn't known how insane it would look for him to spontaneously wrap Roth in the biggest hug, he would've done it and given him a smacking kiss on the jaw to boot. Autumn appeared to be done talking about Vivienne when Roth asked a follow-up question.

"What made Vivi come back here now? I thought she was happy in South Dakota."

Completely oblivious to the way Rhine was hanging on her every word, Autumn answered while plucking another warm yeast roll from the bread basket and slathering butter on it. Rhine gripped his fork to keep himself from urging her to answer more quickly.

He hadn't seen Vivienne in almost three years. He honestly thought he'd gotten over their on-again-off-again fling. Apparently, he hadn't. Not if he was sitting on the edge of his seat with his ears primed like the town gossip, ready to hear the latest on how Mr. Irwin was stepping out on Miss Susie down at the Pick and Save.

"She was...is..."

Autumn paused with her head tilted to one side as she considered her response for a beat, then continued.

"It's not about her not liking it in South Dakota. When she called me the other day to fuss at me, she said she loved it there. But she loves the Sunset Ranch more and wants it to stay in the family."

"Did you tell her I offered to join the Lazy Creek with the Sunset—to keep them from selling it to a stranger?"

Placing her hand on Roth's, Autumn gave it a rub, then patted the back. While Rhinehart found her attempt to soften the blow of rejection touching, Rhine just wanted her to keep talking about Vivienne.

"I told her, Baby. She said it was sweet, but if that

happened, it would be like the Lazy Creek swallowed the Sunset."

Rhine hadn't planned to do more than listen to learn what he could, but the words jumped out of his mouth.

"Since when is Vivienne interested in cows? Horses are her thing."

Lowering his fork, Roth rested his elbow on the table, leaning closer to Rhine.

"Since when do you know what Vivi is into?"

"Vivienne."

Rhine's quick correction of his brother's shortening of Vivienne's name received a quirked eyebrow response from Roth. Rhine didn't answer Roth's challenge of his knowledge of Vivienne. He stared back at his brother for a few beats before Roth rephrased his question.

"Since when do you know what Vivienne is into?"

"Anyone familiar with the Daley family knows Vivienne loves horses. Besides, when I used to do the junior rodeo stuff, she was always hanging around. If you recall, she was one of the youngest barrel racers in her age class the first time she won."

The smile stretching across his brother's face was a little too telling for Rhine's liking. He was happy when Autumn jumped back into the conversation.

"Of course, everyone knows the way Vivi loves horses. Uncle Clint had to drive Princess to South Dakota for her when she decided to stay on longer at the Silver Creek, because she didn't want to be separated from her baby."

"You're right, Sugar. I don't know how I forgot about that."

Autumn patted Roth's hand again.

"I don't know how you forgot either. She said you were the one who told her about the ranch and how much working there helped you when you resigned your commission."

Rhine had done a good job of pushing that little bit of knowledge to the back of his mind. Knowing his brother was the catalyst for Vivienne moving to a tiny town in South Dakota instead of living in the house she owned in Lone Star Ridge stung more than a little. It didn't matter that Roth had no way of knowing he'd encouraged Vivienne to leave Rhine.

Rhine and Vivienne had purposely not told their families about their relationship. Probably because calling it a relationship was a stretch. They had sex. Lots of it. Enthusiastically. Whenever she was in town on leave and when she was in Houston doing one advanced medic training or another.

But a relationship, it was not. Although, when she left the Army for good, Rhine thought it was past time to change their dynamic. Just as he was ready to push the issue, she up and moved to Ironhaven to work on a ranch. Rhine was sure some of her family echoed his thoughts. There was a perfectly good ranch at the end of Daley Road she could work on. Why did she have to move over a thousand miles away?

In the end, nothing either of them said made a difference. Vivienne left. But now...now she was coming back. Rhine didn't really care about the reasons. His focus remained on the results; Vivienne was coming home. And all the lies he'd told himself for the past few years no longer held any strength.

There were some days when Rhine regretted talking his father into keeping the satellite office of Stephens Industries open in Lone Star Ridge. Then there were the days when the view of the nostalgic downtown area offered him the opportunity to glimpse a sight he would've missed if he still worked at the high-rise building in Houston.

Today, not only did he not regret his decision, Rhine patted himself on the back for making it. Not simply the suggestion to his pop, but making it his home base when he took over as CEO. Normally, he didn't spend time gazing out the window. However, he'd just wrapped up a video conference with the marketing team when he glanced away from his monitor.

Hearing about Vivienne's return from Autumn should've prepared him for eventually seeing her. But it hadn't. He didn't recognize the extended-cab pickup truck she got out of, but he'd never forget Vivienne Daley's beautiful face. She'd filled out more since the last time he'd seen her—in all the places he liked.

While she was in the service, she'd complained about the extra things she went through to maintain the Army's weight standards. Now, her five-foot-eight-inch frame carried more ample hips, ass, and fuller legs than before. Her breasts were bigger too. Rhine guessed they'd fill his hands with moderate spillover.

His fingers itched to test his theory. Memories of how well their bodies played together flooded his thoughts as if they'd happened moments ago instead of the years it had been since he'd last touched her. And whatever the actual reasons behind her leaving were, his Rose had blossomed while she was away.

He'd managed not to call when he heard the news of Vivienne's pending return. But seeing her shoved his restraint so far down, he didn't recall the word existed.

On his desk, Rhine's cellphone lay within reach. It seemed to magically appear in his hand as his fingers swiped through to find her name in his contact list. He shoved an earbud into his ear just in time to detect the first ring.

Standing, he moved closer to the window. As the phone rang, he watched her dig into her back pocket. His jaw clenched as he considered she might ignore the call. Even if she'd be within her rights to do so, he wouldn't like that shit. At all.

The tension in his jaw transferred when the ringing stopped, replaced by Vivienne's voice.

"I probably should've expected this call, but I didn't."

"Hello to you too, Rose."

Resting one forearm on the window, Rhine leaned against it, peering down into the street below. He wasn't close enough to catch every micro-expression, but he read her body language pretty well. With the phone pressed against her ear, she turned. If he hadn't known the tempered glass kept anyone from seeing inside, he'd swear she was looking directly at him.

"Are we friends again? People who speak regularly, so that it's not odd when my phone rings and you're on the other end of the call?"

Heat licked up Rhine's neck. As his brain processed what she'd said to him, his feet were already carrying him toward the door and out of his office via the private exit. Her words weren't a deterrent; they were motivators.

"Are you really giving me shit, Rose? Are we pretending you weren't the one who stopped answering my calls? Like you didn't tell me not to come visit you in South Dakota? Or are we revising history to where I'm the one who told you our arrangement was over?"

Since he'd given up his post at the window, he couldn't see her physical response to his comeback. However, at his current pace, he knew she'd be within sight in a few seconds, and he'd be in her space not long after that.

When Vivienne released a huffing breath as she spoke, Rhine understood the phrase his mama had read to him from one of her romance novels. Vivienne's voice was the definition of "much aggrieved."

"Rhine...did you call me to argue? Or was there a particular purpose? I'm guessing you heard I'm moving back to Lone Star."

By the time she'd asked, Rhine was pushing through the door leading from the building. Skirting the side, he crossed the street, walking toward her truck. With her back facing him, she didn't see him coming.

"Rhine? Are you still there?"

Pulling the phone from her ear, she looked at it before putting it back. When she did, he tapped his earbud to end the call.

"No. I'm not still there. I'm right here."

He wondered if her gasp was because of the surprise of his being right behind her or surprise at seeing him at all.

"And I don't plan to argue with you about history. It's done. Can't be changed. No matter how much you want to twist it to suit your narrative."

Tracking Vivienne's eye roll and pursed lips, Rhine closed the distance until barely air separated them.

"Keep rolling your eyes at me, Rose. You know my policy about bratty behavior."

It took everything in Rhine to maintain his posture once her arms brushed against him when she folded them across her middle. A single arched brow climbed her forehead with her attempt to give him a scathing up/down glance.

# Chapter Two

IF VIVIENNE LIVED to be a hundred, she'd probably still be amazed at Rhinehart Stephens' arrogance. How dare he think he could pop back into her life the second she entered town, then act as if she was to blame for them being estranged?

Forcing herself to ignore how delicious he looked in the blue button-down shirt and fitted jeans, she tried to maintain her focus. Although she was certain he saw her from the window of his office, she hadn't consciously parked in his line of sight. It was simply her luck that the Daley Group building was directly across the street from the Stephens Industries satellite office.

"Your *policies...*" Putting air quotes around the word 'policies,' Vivienne continued, "and opinions about my behavior don't mean anything, Rhinehart Stephens."

Pointing to the building, which looked a little too modern for the tiny downtown area, she worked to keep her expression and her voice from showing how affected she was by his nearness.

"And unlike the people who work in that building, you

aren't the boss of me. So, you don't get a say in how I conduct myself."

Irritated at him not only for trying to tell her how she should act but also for throwing her so off balance he could sneak up behind her, Vivienne's frown deepened. When Rhine's expression darkened, she knew she'd hit a nerve. His reaction caused a dual internal response.

He was hot as fuck when he dropped into broody-bossy mode, which was...distracting...for her. But she had to stand her ground. The other side of Vivienne fought to remind her she'd had no intention of resuming their previous friends-with-benefits agreement, no matter how good he was at blowing her back out.

There were many nights she'd lain in bed in her little bungalow in Ironhaven, wishing he were just a call away to put her to sleep by sucking her soul out through her pussy. But...this wasn't then. She had different priorities now. Getting caught up with Rhinehart Stephens wasn't on the agenda.

So, she couldn't give in to him calling her Rose. Nor could she get sidetracked by him standing in front of her looking all ferocious, fine, and fuckable. *Focus, Daley! That's an order!*

Normally, her internal drill sergeant straightened her up, forcing her to power through any situation. This time... Not so much. Especially not when Rhine was standing so close. Looking like that. Smelling soooo good... *Jesus, why did he smell so good?*

He stayed silent for so long after her declaration Vivienne began feeling like she might've won the battle. Wrong. So very wrong. The second she took a small step backward—not ceding ground, simply trying to leave—she found herself caged.

Her own truck kept her from escaping the mountain of man surrounding her. *Why the hell were those Stephens men so damn big?* None of the ingrained combat skills drilled into her mattered with him being so close. So tempting.

"Where do you think you're going, Rose? Think you can just tell me what's what and walk off? Did you forget who I am? What I can do to and with my Sweetie Pie? Because you're acting like you need a reminder."

Vivienne's eyes slid closed without her consent. Why the hell did he have to bring up the nickname he'd given her pussy? It had been cute and funny the first time he'd popped up from between her legs, his chin glistening with her juices, and a wide grin on his face. Declaring the sweetness of her nectar, he'd dubbed her pussy Sweetie Pie from that moment on.

Then, when he wanted to hook up, it wasn't uncommon for him to request a meeting with Sweetie Pie via text message. It used to be cute when he brought it up. But that was before she decided they weren't good together, and she needed to stay away from his big sexy ass. Having her core clench from the memories of all the ways he made it cream wasn't helping the situation.

A deep, fortifying breath provided Vivienne with the oxygen she needed to try to fight this thing between them before it went further off the rails. Slowly, as if she feared doing so would burn her, she raised her hands, placing them on his chest, pressing, trying to move an immovable object.

"I'm acting like a person who has places to be and doesn't have time for whatever this is you think you're doing, Rhinehart. Please move."

Dear Lord, she needed him to move. Touching him had been a mistake. A big one. Although he didn't work the ranch anymore, his body maintained the bulkiness which had made him give up rodeo activities in his youth once it became obvious he'd need to move to steer wrestling instead of bronc riding. And all of that man, so close to her, was fucking with Vivienne's resolve to stay away from Rhinehart Stephens.

"Vivi, Rhine...is everything okay?"

Autumn's voice was the bucket of cold water Vivienne needed to get her to stop considering tossing caution to the wind and climbing Rhine instead of pushing him away. The eyes she used to spend far too much time trying to figure out if they were amber, hazel, or blue bored into her. For a beat, she thought he might ignore Autumn in favor of proving his point.

But he stood up straight, allowing some space between them, giving Vivienne a clear view of her cousin. Vivienne expected her cousin's confused expression. She hadn't told Autumn about her situationship with Rhine.

The only person who knew for certain was Vivienne's best friend, Trent. Since he and his husband were stationed in Colorado, he wasn't likely to tell her family.

Pasting a smile onto her face, Vivienne used the gap Rhinehart created to step aside, closer to her cousin.

"Everything is fine, Tummy. Rhinehart and I were just talking."

Autumn's gaze bounced between the two of them assessingly before stopping on Rhine.

"If you say so, Vivi. Rhine, are you joining us for lunch?"

Before Rhinehart could respond, Vivienne cut in.

"No, he can't. Besides, I wanted to talk to you first. That's why I came early."

Confusion dipped Autumn's brow.

"You need to talk to me? About what?"

Slipping her arm through Autumn's, Vivienne tugged her back toward the Daley Group building.

"I'll tell you when we get to your office."

Hazarding a glance over her shoulder where Rhinehart still

stood next to her pickup, Vivienne attempted to put polite distance between them.

"Bye, Rhinehart. It was...nice...seeing you again. We can catch up another time."

"Sure we can, Rose."

Vivienne recognized the lazy grin stretching his lips, which were framed by a perfectly groomed mustache and beard.

"I'll come back in..." Flipping his wrist, he looked at his watch. "Say... thirty minutes to take you ladies to lunch. There's a new place that just opened off I-10 going toward Katy. I've been meaning to try it."

Autumn's face lit up, making Vivienne want to kick her for not catching a very pointed hint.

"Oh! I've been wanting to go there. Me and Roth keep missing it because of one thing or another."

Placing his fingers on his forehead as if tipping a hat, Rhine tilted his chin down.

"Well, it's a date. I'll see you ladies at noon. I'll drive."

Vivienne, working her mouth like a fish, didn't stop her cousin from bobbing her head in agreement with Rhinehart's insane suggestion. Couldn't she see Vivienne was drowning? Did she not care?

"Okay. We'll see you then. I'd call Roth, but I know they were talking about moving the herd to the northern pasture today, and he's probably up to his elbows in cows."

As they entered the building, not even the blast of cool air could calm the heat Rhine's stare stoked inside Vivienne. She didn't look back at him; it wasn't necessary. She felt the intensity of his gaze from the top of her head to the tips of her toes.

Only after walking farther into the building, when she was certain they were out of his sight, did the feeling calm. Of course, it was then, her once-favorite cousin stopped playing dumb and used the brain that had her graduating at the top of her class and passing the Nevada State Bar on the first try.

Closing the door to her office behind them, Autumn turned, leaning against it with her arms folded.

"So, tell me the truth. What's up with you and Rhine? And don't say 'nothing.' I've never in my life seen you let a man crowd you, unless you wanted him there. And he calls you Rose...!"

Matching Autumn's pose, Vivienne tilted her head, returning her stare.

"Where was all this situational awareness when I was trying to get us in here without committing to a lunch that included more than just me and you?"

Straightening, Autumn moved away from the door. Taking her purse from her shoulder, she placed it on her desk, then leaned against the mahogany surface.

"I asked you if everything was okay. You said yes. What did you expect me to do? Call you a liar?"

"I didn't expect you to invite him to lunch with us. I came to see you. Talk to you. Not..." Vivienne went silent, searching for the words to describe Rhine which wouldn't give her cousin more information than necessary. "Him. He just happened to be there when I pulled up."

It was a lie. But just a tiny white one. Too bad for Vivienne, Autumn already smelled blood.

"Girl, please. No, he wasn't. I saw you pull up when I was walking past the windows. I came back to my office to get my purse. By the time I got it and made it outside, he was there. So, lie to yourself all you want; just don't lie to me."

Rolling her eyes, Vivienne looked away from Autumn's too-knowing stare. Already tired of this conversation, she decided to just change the subject. Waving a hand dismissively, Vivienne sat in one of the moderately comfortable-looking chairs in front of Autumn's desk.

"I didn't come here to talk about Rhinehart Stephens. Like I said outside, I wanted to talk to you about something."

Autumn stared at Vivienne long enough to make her think Autumn was going to keep digging for more info about what was going on with Rhine. She hadn't realized the amount of tension in her shoulders until Autumn relented, asking a non-Rhinehart-related question.

"What did you want to talk about?"

Shoving Rhine as far out of her thoughts as she could, Vivienne shifted to her reasons for needing to see her cousin. Since Autumn returned to living in Lone Star Ridge full-time, she'd become more active in the business their fathers started decades ago. Although she functioned as their corporate attorney, Vivienne was certain Autumn could point her in the right direction.

And she did. Just not in the direction Vivienne thought she would. Definitely not on a path she wanted to take. The chair cushion didn't provide the support she needed, pressing into her back.

"So, you're saying you're not gonna help me? You know if I can't get something going before Grandma Hattie's deadline, she's gonna sell the ranch."

Sitting in the chair opposite her, Autumn leaned over, tapping the back of Vivienne's hand.

"First of all, I didn't say I would not help. What I'm saying is, the Daley Group doesn't offer the services you need to start a therapeutic horse ranch. We can help with equipment, getting the new stables, and things of that nature.

We can probably help with selling off the cattle. But we don't do marketing. Nor do we have the infrastructure to help with the other things you'll need to put your plan into action. The rest..."

Autumn shook her head while wearing an uncomfortable grimace.

"You'll have to get help outside the family. And we both know who you can ask...Rose."

"Don't call me that."

Her mother would've chastised Vivienne for being a grown woman pouting like a child. It didn't stop Vivienne from pursing her lips while hugging herself. Autumn's light giggles weren't helping Vivienne's struggle to be mature.

"Why can't I call you Rose? It's kinda cute. Now, I wanna know the story of how you got the name."

Vivienne barely caught herself before she made a quip about Autumn explaining why Roth called her Sugar. She didn't need to invite her cousin to connect her with Rhinehart in anything similar to the relationship Autumn had with his brother.

"Just don't call me Rose."

Pushing up from the chair, Autumn grabbed her purse from the desk.

"Fine. I'm hungry, and Rhine said he'd be here at noon. It's eleven fifty-five. Let's go."

Vivienne bit back every curse she wanted to utter, then choked them down. It would only put Autumn on her tail even more. She definitely didn't want her spilling the beans to the other cousins... or, heaven forbid, her parents. If Autumn mentioned anything to her father, Vivienne's father would know within minutes. She just hoped neither man was anywhere around when Rhinehart arrived.

# Chapter Three

IT WAS HARD AS HELL, but Rhine managed not to grin like a maniac when Autumn mentioned Vivienne needing his help. Imagine that. His Rose coming back to Lone Star Ridge to save the Sunset Ranch from being sold was shaping up to be just what he needed to get out of the rut he'd fallen into. Business was going well, but the challenge of it had waned.

The mutinous expression on Vivienne's face did nothing to squelch his joy at knowing she needed something only he could help her with. Technically, she could find another company to assist with all the steps she'd have to take to turn a working cattle ranch into the equine haven she had planned.

She could, but she wouldn't. The deadline her grand-mother had given her left little time for her to track one down, obtain a contract, and actually get anything moving toward achieving her goal. Especially considering he'd just learned she didn't have a business plan written out—only ideas and a few notes.

To her credit, she had the names of horse dealers and some connections she'd made in South Dakota to get the animals. Since she'd earned certifications while working at the Silver

Creek Ranch, some customers would follow her to her new location without much need to advertise. To reach new people and get to her target audience, she needed him.

Placing his fork on his empty plate, Rhine leaned away from the table, his gaze fixed on Vivienne. During the entire lunch, she'd only spoken when Autumn prompted her. The request had technically come from Autumn by way of explaining how the Daley Group didn't provide the services Vivienne needed, but Stephens Industries did.

"Rose, are you asking for my help, or is Autumn?"

Was it a dick move to make her speak up and ask for herself? Yes. Did Rhine care as long as it meant she spoke directly to him? No. Autumn's eyes rounded as she stared at her cousin.

Shooting him a glare that probably made many a hardened soldier reconsider their life choices, his Rose pursed her lips then folded her arms. Matching her posture, Rhine tilted his head to one side, lifting a single eyebrow.

The silence crackled with tension while the two had a silent conversation. Their 'relationship' had always been amicable. Until she called things off, they met each other's needs, laughed together, and generally got along. The Vivienne who'd returned to Lone Star Ridge was a version of his Rose he'd only glimpsed when she'd relayed stories of incidents while she served.

Though it didn't put him off. During the time between when she'd walked into the Daley Group building with Autumn and her climbing into the passenger seat of his vehicle, he'd determined there wasn't anything she could do to change his feelings about her. Not even asking him to stop.

His lips twitched watching Vivienne struggle not to curse him out while Autumn gave her the eye, encouraging her to speak up. Suddenly sitting up straight, Vivienne transferred her glare to Autumn.

"Stop kicking me, Tummy."

"Stop being a big baby, Vivi."

Rhine had to bite the inside of his cheek to keep from grinning, observing the scene unfold in front of him. Autumn always seemed so even-keeled, while Vivienne didn't exactly have an opposite personality; they were not the same. With only a year separating them in age, it seemed Autumn was pulling the older cousin card.

Their conversation turned nonverbal for the next couple of minutes, robbing him of further enjoyment from their little tiff, before Vivienne sighed and returned her gaze to Rhine. Briefly, he thought she might continue to hold out. Finally, she unfolded her arms, clasping her hands together in her lap.

"Rhinehart, is it possible someone at Stephens Industries could help me with the logistics of converting Sunset Ranch from a working cattle operation to one that offers equine therapy services and a sanctuary for horses?"

Resting his forearms on the table, Rhine studied her for a second, then dipped his chin.

"Can *someone* at Stephens Industries help you? No."

Autumn's gasp was deep enough to suck the air out of the room.

"Rhine! I can't believe you just said that."

Pushing her chair away from the table, Vivienne placed a hand on Autumn's arm.

"Don't, Tummy. I asked; he said no."

"I didn't say no, Rose."

Not getting up, Rhine kept his eyes on Vivienne.

"I speak three languages, Rhine. 'No', is the same in all of them. I'm positive I heard you correctly."

Allowing his gaze to roam over her, Rhine shook his head.

"I'm just as positive you heard what you wanted to hear. You asked if *someone* at Stephens Industries could help. *Someone* can't. But *I* can."

Shaking her head, Vivienne stood.

"I don't have time to play games, Rhinehart."

Standing, Rhine took her hand in his before she could move.

"Who's playing, Rose? I'm being pretty clear. No faceless, nameless person at S.I. will be assigned to help you. Besides, if I did that, the fees would rack up pretty quickly."

"You think I can't pay?"

Rounding the table completely, Rhine kept his voice low, although he couldn't give two shits if someone heard him.

"I never said you couldn't pay."

"What are you saying then?"

"I'm saying if we go the route you're implying, it involves contracts, a team, and a significant amount of money."

Rolling her eyes, Vivienne huffed.

"Why do you keep saying the same thing while thinking it means something else? You're still implying I don't have the money to pay. I assure you, I do. I don't need a free ride."

Lowering his head to speak directly into her ear, Rhine released her hand, sliding an arm around her waist.

"No ride is ever free, Rose. But if anyone is getting ridden, it'll be me."

The heat blazing from Vivienne's eyes was hot enough to burn him where he stood. Rhine met her stare without flinching. He knew she didn't need him to explain further. The only way she'd get help from Stephens Industries would be through him.

Not for a second did Rhine consider the years he'd avoided being directly involved in ranching life. Working for the company kept him from dealing with the daily activities involved in running a ranch.

If he helped Vivienne, and he damn well intended to help her, it couldn't be done peripherally. He'd have to be the team he refused to assign her from the company. It would mean long hours and many trips to the ranch and other places to get everything she needed in the time she had left.

And... since it had taken her a few weeks to relocate from Ironhaven, she'd already lost a month. She couldn't afford to turn him down. They both knew it. When her teeth came down on her bottom lip, Rhinehart straightened up but didn't loosen his hold on her waist.

Autumn's voice sliced through their silent standoff.

"Ummm... do you two need to speak privately somewhere?"

Without diverting his attention to his soon-to-be sister-in-law, Rhine kept Vivienne in his hold when she attempted to move away.

"Naw, Autumn. We're fine. Aren't we, Rose?"

Flexing his fingertips into the small of her back earned Rhine a side-eye glance before Vivienne turned to her cousin.

"It's all good, Tummy. But I'm sure you need to get back to the office. So, we should probably get the check."

With a shake of his head, Rhine finally released his hold on Vivienne, stepping behind Autumn's chair.

"Don't worry about the check. It's taken care of."

After he helped Autumn from her seat, Rhine returned to Vivienne's side, placing a hand on the small of her back. When she didn't try to pull away, he pressed his thumb against her spine, rubbing in a small circle. For a split second, her steps halted, but she quickly seemed to find her footing.

Neither woman complained about his taking over in settling the bill. Following a short, silent battle of wills between the cousins over Vivienne attempting to sit in the rear passenger seat, they rode back in relative silence. Only the radio competed with the hum of the engine.

Stopping the vehicle in front of the Daley Group building, Rhine cut the engine and stepped out to open the door for Autumn. With a questioning expression on her face, she tilted her head toward his hand on the front passenger door. He knew without looking that Vivienne was glaring at him. He also knew, if he didn't keep his hand on the door, she'd open it and hop out. He wasn't nearly done with her.

Returning Autumn's silent question with lifted eyebrows, Rhine waited for her to say something. The slight whir of the window lowering got both of their attention.

"Can you let me out, please?"

The words she used were polite, but Vivienne's tone wasn't close to being cordial.

"Did you forget we needed to talk, Rose?"

Not waiting for Vivienne to answer, he glanced at Autumn.

"You heading back into the office, Autumn?"

Rhine almost asked if she needed anything else from Vivienne but stopped. Feelings of selfishness kept him from offering a second of her time to anyone else.

Autumn's gaze bounced between them before she nodded.

"Yeah... I have a meeting this afternoon."

Taking one step back, she looked at her cousin.

"Are you good, Vivi?"

Gritting his teeth against snapping, Rhine stared at Vivienne, silently daring her to get her cousin in the middle of their business. Her chin jutted out slightly when her eyes left his to focus on Autumn.

"I'm good."

In his periphery, Rhine noted Autumn slowly backing away.

"Okay. Well, call me later. Maybe we can have a girls' night or something. Catch up."

Rhine wasn't totally fluent in woman-speak, but he understood what Autumn wasn't saying. She wanted to know what was going on between him and Vivienne. Avoiding his gaze, Vivienne gave her cousin a tight smile.

"Yeah. We should do that. I'll call you."

While saying goodbye to her cousin, Vivienne continued to deny him eye contact. Instead, she looked straight ahead. Rhine didn't care, so long as she didn't jump out the second he let go of the door.

"Let up the window, Rose."

Before he finished speaking, the window rolled up between them. Grinning, Rhine dipped his chin. He wasn't really into spanking, but it seemed like his Rose was angling for one. To his own ears, Rhine's chuckle held a sinister edge.

Rounding the front of the SUV, he got in before she got any ideas about locking him out. He didn't have time to put the vehicle in gear before it seemed she lost her internal battle.

"You know you could've just asked me to stay in the car. You didn't have to hold me inside like some unruly child."

"Don't act like an unruly child, and I won't treat you like one."

Ignoring her sharp inhale, he made a U-turn, driving toward the attached parking of his office building. Neither of them spoke until he came to a stop in his designated parking space. But it wasn't anything more than his telling her not to move as he got out to open her door.

With a hand at the small of her back, he led her into the building and to his office. If his assistant had any thoughts about Vivienne's presence, she kept them to herself.

Once they were inside with the door firmly closed, Vivienne stepped away from him. Against what his hands wanted him to do, Rhine let her go.

Vivienne stopped in front of the small conference table on the opposite side of the room. Carefully observing her, Rhine waited. It was a brief wait. Releasing a slow breath, Vivienne lifted her hands with her palms outward.

"Listen...I'm not ungrateful for you agreeing to help me. But it doesn't mean..."

Breaking eye contact with him, Vivienne stared at the bookshelf as if it held the rest of her sentence hostage. Rhine didn't like where it sounded like her sentence was going. Crossing the room in three long strides, he stood in front of her in less than two seconds.

"It doesn't mean what, Rose?"

As much as he wanted to wrap his arms around her and hold her tightly to his chest, Rhine kept himself from doing it. He was in her space, breathing her air. Yet he didn't touch her.

Her tongue peeked from her mouth, wetting her bottom lip, making him jealous of the privilege. Although she squinted a little each time he called her Rose, she didn't ask him to stop. That was good, because he wasn't sure he could respect the boundary.

# Chapter Four

VIVIENNE WASN'T WEAK. She didn't cower to anyone—especially not to some man. And, technically, she wasn't cowering to Rhinehart. She was simply choosing her words carefully. Setting him off wouldn't help her achieve her goal. *Remember the goal* was on repeat in her head while she stared into the face of the man who'd come closer than anyone to making her wish for a different life.

A life where seeing too much in war hadn't scarred her. Where she hadn't battled with her inner demons until she thought it might be better to let them win rather than suffer the way she had. Taking Roth's recommendation and going to Silver Creek had saved more than her sanity.

But if she'd attempted to hold on to Rhinehart...Vivienne didn't want to think of what she might have done to him if they'd tried to be more than fuck buddies. Yet now he stood before her—invading her space. Making her think things... things like, what if she was wrong? What if there had been a different way for her to climb out of the pit she'd fallen into when she left the military?

A vigorous mental shake was required for Vivienne to get

herself together enough to respond to Rhinehart's question and not to his presence. Still...the words left her far softer than they'd appeared in her head.

"It doesn't mean you get to control me."

The more she spoke, the prouder Vivienne became of the strength returning to her voice.

"You can't just pick me up and move me where you want, like I'm some puppet on a string."

Instead of responding immediately, he stepped closer. The tips of his boots met the ends of hers. Vivienne steeled her spine and held her breath. He was too close. Bringing his scent into her nostrils and the heat of his body into her space was too much. However, she refused to back down. Tilting her chin, she met his hard stare with one of her own.

"Who said I was trying to control you, Rose?"

"It's not what you said, Rhine. It's what you're doing. I'm not too proud to accept help to save my ranch. But you've gotta stop all..." Waving her hand in the tiny space between them, she continued, "this stuff. We're not picking up where we left off."

Vivienne fought to keep her eyes open when the warmth of his large hand engulfed hers. Her tugging attempt to free herself was a waste of energy—especially once Rhine leaned down, speaking to her in his unnecessarily deep, sexy timbre.

"I ain't trying to pick up where we left off. I told you; the past is done. But you ain't gonna act like we don't mean something to each other either. And if you want my help, it involves this. You being near me. Me being near you. Working together."

*Why was it so hot in here?* The sudden increase in temperature was likely in Vivienne's head, but the sweat beading on her nose wasn't fake.

"I...uh..."

Clearing her throat, Vivienne tried to hear her drill

sergeant telling her to get her shit together, but the fog Rhine's nearness created was like top-tier earplugs shoved into her ears.

"How is this working together?"

Straightening her shoulders, Vivienne couldn't have been prouder that she'd been able to complete a coherent sentence with him looking at her with his mystery-colored eyes.

The hand he placed at the small of her back had turned her body into her betrayer. It automatically melted into his, pressing her breasts into him—allowing her to feel all of him against her.

"This..."

Rhine traced one thick finger along the sliver of skin exposed by the neck of her blouse.

"This is whatever we say it is, Rose. But I think I know what you need."

"Ex—"

When he swallowed her question with his kiss, Vivienne couldn't fault her body's response. It was sexy muscle memory, and she was a starving woman. A low, rumbling groan preceded Rhinehart grabbing her ass in both of his large hands, lifting her off her feet.

Any protests she had, or thoughts of resistance, fled as he walked them across the room. The click of the lock engaging barely reached her ears as she tilted her head to one side. Enjoying the feel of his low beard abrading her skin where he rained kisses on her neck, Vivienne couldn't focus on anything beyond the fire Rhine set blazing inside her.

Cool air brought with it goose pimples, but there was little time for it to register before the soft leather of the sofa met her bare back. If she'd been concerned about how he'd respond to her weight gain, Rhine quickly put the question to rest.

"Look at you, Rose. You're so fucking gorgeous."

He'd always been generous with his praise. Coupled with the near-worshipful quality of his kisses and touches, Vivienne was aroused enough to forget they were in his office in the middle of a workday.

"Oh...Hart..."

The light scrape of his beard as he took her nipple into his mouth made her slide her fingers into his hair, gripping the short strands while squirming against the cushions beneath her. Rhine's hand at her hip didn't stop her movements. They both knew what she wanted. His weight wasn't pressing her into the couch, but her body remembered how it felt and wanted it again.

The rumble of Rhinehart's voice sent tingles through Vivienne, even though she couldn't understand what he said. A second later, her lower half felt the same chill before his warmth was there. How the hell he'd gotten her boots and pants off so quickly, she had no idea. It was a mystery for another time.

At present, the scuffing scrape of his facial hair tickled her inner thighs, and all Vivienne's thoughts went to what he planned next. This time when he spoke, she caught it. Only he wasn't talking to her. At least not to her face.

"It's been too long, Sweetie Pie. Just know it wasn't my fault. But I'm gonna make it all better for you."

Anyone else holding a full-on conversation with her pussy would've made Vivienne dry as a bone. When Rhine did it, she wanted to shove his head closer until not even air separated his mouth from her slick center.

Once he stopped talking, and pulled her panties to the side to access her aching core, Vivienne ceased to think—only feel. His greedy moans vibrated through her, sending her arousal through the roof. She gave no thought to whether the closed door blocked others from hearing them.

"Oh! Hart!"

His name, a gasp, whisper-screamed into the room when he unerringly found her clit and sucked it into his talented mouth, lashing it with his tongue. Without breaking contact with her mons, he pried her fingers from his hair, placing them on her breasts, silently encouraging her to squeeze them.

Denying him wasn't a question in her mind. She knew how hot he found it when she self-pleasured. It made him work even harder to bring her to orgasm. Whether it was the time since they'd last been together or their explosive chemistry, Vivienne crested into orgasm a few moments later with Rhinehart's name on her lips.

Her heavy breathing was the only sound in the room until he started talking to Sweetie Pie again.

"Such a good girl. Giving me your sweet cream. I've got a reward for you."

Through partially lowered lids, Vivienne watched him rise from between her thighs and sit on the sofa. The clinking sound of his belt buckle should've made her pull herself together and get out of there. Instead, she licked her lips when his big dick appeared in the opening of his jeans.

His shirt was more than halfway unbuttoned, but he didn't shrug it off. The fitted jeans were only lowered enough for him to release Vivi's old friend. Long, with ample girth, the tip of his cock glistened. Her tongue peeked from between her lips, remembering his taste.

"Stop looking at him like that. It's riding time. You can kiss him later."

If she'd been more in control, Vivienne would've had a snappy comeback. Not this time. This time, her body was running things. It explained where she found the energy to straddle his lap and slide down onto his thickness.

"Ah!"

Shocked at the mild sting from the smack to her bottom, Vivienne's eyes popped open to see Rhine's gaze focused on where their bodies joined. She'd stopped halfway, unable to take him all in one stroke.

"Sweetie Pie can take it, Rose. Let her have all of it."

Once he looked up at her, Vivienne forgot about her momentary discomfort. Her muscles relaxed, allowing her to glide the rest of the way until he was embedded inside her.

"Fuck...Hart."

"Yeah, Baby. I know."

The warmth of his large hands rubbing her ass while his thickness filled her to the brim was nearly overwhelming. But Vivienne needed more. Lifting slightly, she started a rhythm which had her racing toward release too soon. Rhine didn't help with the things he said.

Speaking directly into her ear, he alternated between squeezing her ass and tweaking her nipples while peppering her with kisses.

"That's it, Rose. Ride. Take what you and Sweetie Pie need. What you've been missing."

When he started in about it being too long and how he was going to fill her up with every drop of his cum, Vivienne lost touch with reality. She became a collection of nerve endings overwhelmed with pleasure.

She should've expected it, but her orgasm caught her off guard, tossing her into oblivion. Stars burst behind her eyelids. Her shortened version of Rhinehart's name was on her lips before he swallowed it with a scorching kiss.

Strong arms kept her anchored to him as he powered up into her slick sheath before joining her in orgasm land with a grunting growl. Vivienne didn't bother to inspect the damage, but she was certain he kept his word, and she was going to be a sticky mess.

Limply leaning into Rhine, she tried to catch her breath. His broad chest lifted and lowered beneath her cheek, with sweat causing his shirt to cling more tightly to it.

Quiet moments passed with him rubbing his hands up and down her back, giving gentle squeezes to her ass. Vivienne wouldn't ask him, but she got the feeling he enjoyed how much bigger it was now—although it had never been small.

Eventually, the realization of what they'd done filtered to the forefront of Vivienne's thoughts. Rhine's hold on her tightened when she sat up straight.

"What's wrong?"

The dip of his brow gave him a dark, roguish look when combined with his disheveled hair. Under different circumstances, she might've smiled at her handiwork, tousling the dark strands. Instead, she was internally cringing. Shifting her stare to a benign button on his mostly open shirt, questions filled her head.

How the hell had she managed to get fucked by Rhinehart Stephens less than two hours after seeing him for the first time in years? Who does that? So caught up in her thoughts, she didn't reply to Rhine's question. The tips of his fingers flexed into her lower back and butt, bringing her gaze to his face.

"Rose...what's wrong, Baby?"

Pushing against his chest, she tried to separate from him again, but his hold remained, keeping her in place.

"Vivienne?"

Why did it ping her heart a little for him to use her given name?

"I need to go. Let me up, please."

"First, tell me why you're looking like that."

Vivienne's eyebrows climbed her forehead.

"You're not serious..."

When Rhine didn't respond, she shook her head.

"You are, aren't you? You don't see anything wrong with what just happened. In your office. In the middle of a workday. With your employees right outside that door."

When he shrugged, she had a strong desire to shove his broad shoulders and push him down. Except he was already down, and she was on top of him, with his dick still inside her.

"It's not like they have their ears pressed to the door listening. Besides, my office is soundproof."

Of course it was. Rolling her eyes, Vivienne gave pulling away another try.

"Can you let me up, please?"

"Can you be honest with me for once?"

Vivienne stared at him in disbelief.

"Excuse me? What do you mean by that? I'm not a liar."

Rhine's firm hold on her hips, keeping them connected, didn't lessen during their exchange. In addition to his unwillingness to release her, he started moving his thumbs in distracting circles. Vivienne wouldn't allow his caress to soften her. No one called her a liar.

"I never said you were a liar, Rose. You avoid—which doesn't sit right with me either."

Fuck. He had her there. Staring at him mutely, Vivienne was suddenly acutely aware of her nakedness. Crossing her arms over her breasts didn't help much, but it was something.

When Rhine shrugged out of his shirt and draped it around her shoulders, it was difficult not to lift the material to her nose to sniff his scent. It wasn't necessary since he surrounded her. Reaching deep inside, she found what her Granny called her 'pluck.'

"I wouldn't need your shirt if you'd let me up."

"Give me answers first. Then you can have your clothes."

Vivienne's mouth dropped open. The set of his jaw conveyed the seriousness of Rhine's declaration.

*You've stepped in it this time, Daley.*

# Chapter Five

RHINE KNEW he was pushing his luck, but it didn't stop him. Not even the distraction of having his dick still firmly embedded inside her slick walls would keep him from making her talk. He had a good idea of why she'd attempted to bolt. He simply wanted her to admit it.

More than that, he wanted the real reason she didn't want to pick up where they left off. He didn't want to either, but he wanted to know her reasons. His were clear. He'd shown it with his behavior in front of Autumn. Going forward, anything between him and Vivienne wouldn't be a secret. Everyone—including their families—would know about it.

He also knew there was more to her trying to get up than worry about his employees hearing them or guessing what happened. Normally, he'd never lock his door to have sex in his office. But since he held majority shares in Stephens Industries, he owned this building and the company. So, he'd do whatever the hell he wanted.

"Rhine... Can we not? I have other things to do today."

Holding onto her lush hips, with his fingertips grazing her ass, Rhine mentally appreciated their ampleness while dissecting her words and demeanor. Obviously, Vivienne was grasping at straws.

"Things like what? I thought the main thing on your agenda was getting started with what you need for the ranch."

"It is. I told Clay I'd meet him."

"Who's Clay?"

Rhine managed to keep his follow-up questions in his head. Because why the fuck was she in his lap, full of his cock, speaking another man's name?

"He works with Herb at the Sunset. Until Granny started talking about selling, Herb was training him to take over the foreman job."

Understanding didn't make Rhine any less tense. He knew Herb. Herb was a sixty-two-year-old, happily married man. Clay. Rhine didn't know him; so, he didn't trust him.

"Why are you meeting with him and not Herb?"

"Herb's not around; he went to visit his daughter."

She shifted again, and Rhine clamped his hold tighter. The more she wiggled, the more it reminded his dick of being inside her slick walls. Not having gone completely soft after he came, it hardened again. *Stop that shit.*

"Seriously, Rhine. I need to go."

As much as he didn't want to, Rhine adjusted his hold, helping her to her feet. Magnetically, the apex of her thighs drew his gaze. Seeing the shine of their combined juices there didn't help him talk his cock out of trying for another round.

But he ignored it. Instead, he helped her gather her clothes before showing her to his private bathroom. Reaching into the stall, he flicked the knobs on the shower. Soon, the patter of water hitting the tiles was the dominant sound in the room.

When he looked back at Vivienne, she was slipping her arms into her bra straps.

"What are you doing, Rose?"

"There's no way in hell I'm getting in that shower with you. I told you; I have stuff to do."

When he took a step toward her, she took one back, shaking her head. The shaking became more vigorous the closer he got. Each excuse she gave was batted down.

"I don't have a shower cap. My hair will get wet."

Rhine reached into the cabinet, producing a shower cap.

"You know I can't bathe with just any kind of soap."

"No problem, Rose."

Reaching back into the same cabinet, Rhine pulled out a basket filled with woman-friendly products.

"How would it look for me to walk out of here smelling like I just showered?"

Rhine's lips tilted at her last flimsy excuse.

"How would it look for you to walk out of here smelling like sex? Now, I don't mind another man knowing your needs are already being met. But do you really want everyone to wonder what we did in here or know for sure we just finished fucking?"

A few minutes later, they were both in the shower while Rhine graciously assisted Vivienne by washing her back. The conversation he had with his cock made him feel like an addict negotiating a deal to keep from being forcefully placed into rehab. However, he managed not to bend Vivienne over and slide inside her so he could watch her plump ass jiggle while he stroked into her.

*Soon*. Not today. But soon.

When they were done, Rhine made certain they set an actual appointment to discuss things and get the ball rolling. As he escorted her from the office, they stopped at his assistant's desk. He wanted to be certain Claudette knew Vivienne's face and name.

Despite the concerns his Rose voiced inside his office, no one would know from looking at her that she was experiencing the least bit of discomfort with the situation. Once they reached her pickup, Rhine placed his hand on the door before she could get inside.

"Rhine..."

"Shhh, Rose. I'm not trying to stop you from leaving. I just want a second."

The big brown eyes that had haunted his dreams stared up at him expectantly.

"I'll call you when I'm done for the day."

"Rhine, that's unnecessary."

Rhine's brow dipped. Pulling on the handle, he opened the door.

"Neither of us has time to get into the bullshit you just said. So, I'm not gonna start. Get in."

Once she was inside with her safety belt buckled, he leaned into the doorframe, snagging her lips in a quick kiss. Then he stepped back.

"I'll call you later."

Rhine tapped his fingers against the steering wheel. One shower and four hours later, he swore Vivienne's scent lingered on his skin. He didn't mind—other than it having the unfortunate side effect of him getting hard as granite in the middle of a meeting. Good thing for him the meeting was over video, and they could only see the upper half of his body.

When he'd left his office, his plan was to drive to his place, call Vivienne, and have some dinner. Instead of doing either of those things, he sent Vivienne a text. After thirty minutes of no response, he was back in his truck heading toward Daley Road.

This was crazy and borderline stalkerish. Yet, he didn't turn around. Before he reached Vivienne's place, he spied the pickup from earlier parked in front of the Daley family house. Without a thought, he left the main road.

The setting sun shining directly into his face kept him from seeing too far beyond the front of his vehicle until he was closer to the house. Then, he saw Miss Hattie standing on her screened in front porch. She had both hands on her hips as she stood in front of the see through door.

Knowing Vivienne's grandmother would have questions didn't stop him. Rhine parked next to Vivienne's truck, shut off his engine, put his Cattleman-style hat on his head, and stepped out. Gravel crunched beneath his boots as he made his way around the front.

"Hey there, Rhinehart Stephens. Fancy seeing you here."

Accustomed to Miss Hattie's straightforward ways, Rhine smiled, tipping his hat.

"Good evening, Miss Hattie. How are you?"

"I'm doing good for an old lady."

Rhine glanced around as he approached her, wondering where Vivienne was but not asking. Although seeing her truck was the reason he stopped by, he wouldn't be rude to Miss Hattie. Besides, if he found out Vivienne was still out on the land with Clay, he was not sure how he'd respond. It was better to play nice with her grandmother.

"You're not old, Miss Hattie. What is it they say?"

Finally reaching the porch, Rhine climbed the stairs. Opening the door, he leaned over and kissed her cheek.

"You're seasoned."

While stepping back to let him inside, Miss Hattie smiled, giving him an ineffective swat to his chest, her cheeks lifted in a blush.

"You go on with your slick talk, Rhine!"

"What? It's the truth."

Stepping back so she wouldn't have to crane her neck to

look up at him, Rhine leaned against the post opposite where she stood.

"True to who? I'm eighty-four years old, so any seasoning I have has expired."

Chuckling, Rhine shook his head.

"Miss Hattie, you have a way with words, but I stand by what I said. I don't know many eighty-four-year-olds who look half as good as you."

"That's because most of them are dead."

Waving off any counter-response he had, she pierced him with a knowing stare.

"I'm not one to complain about visitors, but something tells me you aren't here for me."

He was caught. However, it didn't make Rhine admit he was only there because of Vivienne.

"Now, Miss Hattie, you act like I never visit."

"I didn't say that. But it's a weekday. Usually, your visits are on the weekend or Sunday afternoons."

It wasn't necessarily a secret, but Rhine didn't broadcast his occasional visits to the Daleys or the Stephens. The creek separated their land, but the tract where Rhine's home sat was closer than Roth's to the main house.

Sometime after Vivienne left for South Dakota, he found himself driving on Daley Road. Miss Hattie had been taking a walk. Rhine slowed to check on her and ended up driving her back home. With Roth and Nick being best friends, Rhine wasn't unfamiliar with Miss Hattie, but their one-on-one interactions had been minimal until that day.

He never made it to Vivienne's empty house. But it was okay. Following their brief chat, he developed a routine of stopping by on the weekends for short visits with Miss Hattie.

"Well, this time I'm here on a Tuesday. Is that alright?"

Raking her sharp gaze over him, she nodded with pursed lips.

"Mhm."

A second later, she looked toward the front door.

"Vivi! You have company."

Rhine stood up straight, extending one hand toward her. "Now, Miss Hattie…"

Waving him off, she gifted him with her patented side-eye. "Don't play me, Rhinehart Stephens."

Before he could respond, the tempered glass door swung open, and Vivienne stepped out onto the porch.

"Granny, what do—?"

Wide-eyed and open-mouthed, Vivienne didn't finish her sentence. Rhine didn't have to think too hard about why. She stood transfixed in the open doorway with a disbelieving stare.

"Close the door, Vivi. You're letting flies into my house. I'll be chasing them for the next two days."

Rhine watched as Vivienne robotically followed her grandmother's instructions. He never took his eyes off her, and she didn't step out farther than necessary for the door to close behind her. She closed her mouth, but her wide-eyed stare never left Rhine's face—until her grandmother spoke again.

"Since you're here, Rhine, are you joining us for supper? There's plenty."

Vivienne's gaze swung to her grandma so quickly, it wouldn't surprise Rhine if she'd made herself dizzy.

"Granny, I'm sure Rhinehart has other things to do, and he's probably already eaten."

"Naw…I don't. And I haven't had supper yet."

Ignoring Vivienne's pointed glare, he opened the door. She stepped aside for her grandma to enter first, then scowled at Rhine some more as he waited for her to follow. Leaning in as she passed, he couldn't stop himself from teasing her a little.

"Clear up your face, Rose. Unless you want me to clear it up for you."

Instead of replying, she huffed, then stalked past him. A

swat to her ass was a mandatory response for her sass, and Rhine didn't hold back. He only made certain Miss Hattie was far enough away not to see it. Vivienne whirled around so quickly they nearly collided.

"Rhinehart Stephens! You stop it."

Hissing and pointing her finger into his chest, Vivienne looked like a fierce little kitten. Rhine smiled even wider.

"Come on, Rose. Your granny is waiting. If it makes you feel better, you can spank my ass later."

Her mouth dropped open, then she snapped it closed, narrowing her eyes.

"I don't like you."

"I don't believe you, but we'll talk about that later too."

Nudging her toward the dining room, Rhine looked up just in time to see Miss Hattie peek back into the hallway.

"Are y'all coming or do you intend to stay in my foyer playing kissy-face?"

"Granny!"

The look of fake innocence on Miss Hattie's face was enough to send Rhine into a fit of laughter. He barely held it together while Vivienne tried to divert attention from their little skirmish.

"Girl, I was born at night. Not last night. Now, come on in here and finish setting the table."

# Chapter Six

VIVIENNE COULDN'T BELIEVE Rhine had just sauntered up to her grandmother's front door and invited himself to dinner. Okay...so maybe Grandma Hattie invited him. But Vivienne was positive she wouldn't have extended the invitation if he wasn't standing right there.

She couldn't imagine her granny calling Rhine up to invite him to dinner on a Tuesday evening. Heck, she barely got an invitation herself. After riding around the property with Clay, Vivienne had come back to the main house to check on her granny and found her in the kitchen cooking. It wasn't on the scale of Sunday dinner, but it was close.

The second Vivienne entered the kitchen, her granny put her to work and told her she might as well help if she was planning to stay. She hadn't thought about her last meal of the day until Grandma Hattie brought it up. Vivienne was having a hard enough time maintaining focus after her *encounter* with Rhine in his office.

Now, she had to sit next to him at the smaller table in her granny's kitchen, pretending her body wasn't throbbing with the memory of what they'd done together just hours ago.

Completely oblivious, after blessing the food, during which Vivienne was forced to endure holding Rhine's hand, Grandma Hattie chattered away. She dished herself a helping of mashed potatoes, then passed the bowl to Rhine.

"Vivi, did Pam tell you what Carla and the Ladies' Auxiliary are planning this year?"

Vivienne tuned back into the conversation in time to hear her grandma's question. She cringed at the idea of what those ladies had dreamed up this time. She'd narrowly escaped the auction last year. It never seemed to dawn on any of them how antiquated those things were. Not to mention the implications of men buying women. It was a sticky ball of 'not touching that' Vivienne wanted to steer clear of. But her granny had asked a question.

"No, ma'am. Mama hasn't said anything to me about the Ladies' Auxiliary."

Vivienne's mother wasn't a member. However, Lone Star Ridge was a small town. Gossip was how people passed the time; so, her mama probably knew the details of every meeting less than an hour after it ended.

"Well, I'm surprised she didn't give you the heads-up."

Before Vivienne could ask why she'd need to be warned, Rhine interjected.

"The heads-up about what, Miss Hattie? They aren't trying to have another one of those date auctions, are they?"

Grandma Hattie paused with a spoonful of green beans hovering over her plate. Her gaze lifted to Rhine's borderline fierce expression, then she continued to serve herself.

"Naw. Not this time. Although, I'm thinking Carla and Virginia are happy about the outcome of the last one with Tummy and Roth getting together.

But this time they're doing something with business-people and professionals. Something about people bidding on having an expert for a day. Or something like that. I was only half-listening until Carla mentioned talking to Pam to see if Vivi was going to be home in time."

Vivienne tried to ignore how the set of Rhine's jaw hadn't relaxed as they listened to her grandmother. His entire body seemed stiffer. She really wanted to change the topic of conversation, but she knew she couldn't rush her granny.

"What does that have to do with me, Grandma?"

"I guess they're thinking you can offer something like the work you did on the ranch in South Dakota. I don't know. You'd have to ask Carla."

Vivienne shook her head.

"The work I did up there takes more than a day. It can take anywhere from weeks to months to gain a horse's trust. I know some people call us horse whisperers, but it's not just walking into a paddock and talking sweet to a horse. There's a process."

Flipping her hand in Vivienne's direction, Grandma Hattie picked up her fork, stabbing a few beans onto the tines.

"Little Girl, I know that. I'm just telling you what I heard. I'm not in it. Just consider yourself warned."

The warmth of Rhine's hand penetrated Vivienne's jeans. She barely kept herself from jumping when it made contact. Glancing at him, Rhine's stare held her captive.

"Eat your supper before it gets cold, Rose."

Biting back the impulse to tell him not to call her that in front of her granny, Vivienne finally looked at her plate. She hadn't touched a single serving dish, but her plate had a portion of each of the offerings on it, except the steamed carrots. She didn't like them.

Rhine had prepared her plate without saying a word, keeping in mind her likes and dislikes. With the way her tongue felt, she was certain it would tangle any words she attempted. So, Vivienne simply picked up her fork, blindly stabbing at the roasted pork.

The rest of the meal passed with Rhine making conversation with her grandmother while Vivienne participated just enough to keep Grandma Hattie from calling her out for being rude. Once it was over, Rhine cleared the table while Vivienne started the water in the sink. Her granny still refused to use her dishwasher or allow anyone else to use it.

Try as she might, Vivienne couldn't ignore how seamlessly they worked together. In less than thirty minutes, they had completed the task and packed away the leftovers, at which point Grandma Hattie made no secret about wanting them to take their leave. Her shows were coming on, and she liked to watch them uninterrupted.

"Okay, Granny. I'll probably be back tomorrow. Clay and I didn't get done today. The ATV got low on fuel. We'll take horses tomorrow; Princess needs the exercise."

Giving her a hug, her grandma kissed Vivienne's cheek while ushering her toward the front door.

"Whatever you say, Baby. You know I'll be here."

Although she was certain he hadn't pressed himself against her, the heat of Rhine's body bathed Vivienne's back, reminding her of his presence—as if she could forget. He reached past her to extend his goodnights to her grandmother.

Once the door was closed between them and Grandma Hattie, Vivienne picked up her pace. Her attempt to put space between them earned her Rhine's voice growling in her ear.

"Are you trying to run from me, Rose? You have to know it's not gonna work. I know where you live, and I also know where you hide the spare key."

Glancing up over her shoulder, Vivienne continued toward her truck.

"No one is running from you, Rhinehart Stephens. I'm simply leaving my granny's house."

Rhine's reply held dark, decadent promises—promises Vivienne had to remind her lady bits they didn't come home to partake in. This was about saving the Sunset Ranch, not having Rhine Stephens scratch her itch.

"Whatever you have to tell yourself, Rose."

When he next spoke, Vivienne had her fingers wrapped around the handle of her car door. Rhine pressed his big hand against the side, keeping the door closed. This time, when she felt his body heat, he was definitely pressed against her.

"I wonder when you started lying to yourself so much. Was it before or after you left Lone Star? I'm thinking it was before. I'm thinking it's one reason you left...lies ... the ones you told yourself, believing they were true."

The moonlight allowed her to see their reflections in the car window. They were in shadow. However, she didn't need to see him in daylight to read his expression. He had questions —ones he was determined to have answered.

"Rhine...can we not do this right now? If we stay out here much longer, Grandma Hattie is going to think something is wrong."

Rhine's other hand gripped Vivienne's hip, pulling her back flush against his front.

"You get a reprieve. But only for as long as it takes for us to drive to your place."

With two taps to her hip, he pried her fingers from the door handle, then opened it. Once she was inside, he leaned over her, snapping her seat belt closed. She wanted to tell him she could buckle herself in, but she didn't. Instead, she watched the set of his jaw, knowing whatever time she thought she had was up. It was T-minus fifteen seconds, and she needed to get her shit together before dealing with him about their personal issues.

During the short drive from her granny's house to her own, Vivienne considered, then discarded possible avenues she could take to avoid the pending conversation with Rhine. As much as she'd healed over the past couple of years, she wasn't sure she was ready for that talk. Not yet.

Vivienne didn't say a word when Rhine parked his truck in the space next to hers in the garage. Although she'd been home for less than two days, there were no boxes or containers clogging up the area. She hadn't acquired many things while she was in South Dakota. The bungalow she rented came furnished. So, she had only her clothing, personal effects, and Princess.

Her horse was in the barn with the others at Sunset, snug in her stall. It hadn't taken long to unpack her clothing and other things. She was grateful to her mother for having the place cleaned and aired out before she arrived.

Before she could step down from the cab of her truck, Rhine was next to her door. Their gazes clashed through the glass before she released the lock, allowing him to open the door. Neither of them spoke until they crossed the threshold, entering the laundry room, which doubled as a mudroom.

"If I hadn't seen you today when you parked in front of the Daley Group, would you have called me? Let me know you were home?"

The intensity of his stare, combined with his questions, was enough to make Vivienne avert her eyes. Avoiding visual contact didn't help her galloping heart. Slipping off her boots, she placed them on the rack, thankful he didn't try to stop her from moving farther into the house.

"I've got all night for you to talk to me, Rose. But we're gonna talk."

Now standing closer to the entryway leading to the hall, Vivienne watched Rhine tug off his boots before placing them on the rack next to hers. It was impossible for her to miss the stark contrast between the size of his compared to hers. Both were custom designs from Ryker's company, *Booted*.

When Rhine stood at his full height, he stared at her for a

beat before stretching one long, beefy arm out toward the doorway behind her.

"After you."

The feeling in Vivienne's stomach wasn't the butterflies of arousal or awareness. It was a ball of dread. *Was there a way to avoid this conversation? God, she hoped so.*

# Chapter Seven

KNOWING he was pushing things with Vivienne didn't make Rhine back off. He honestly wasn't sure if he could. He'd told himself seeking her out after work had to do with getting started on what she needed for the transition of the Sunset. While he'd accused her of lying to herself, he'd told himself a whopper the size of Texas.

He wanted far more than to get started on a strategy for her success. Rhine wanted her. All of her. Not just what they had before—stolen moments where he came to her place or she came to his, always under the cover of night.

Their only daytime trysts happened when they were both in Houston. His condo there wasn't near any of his family or hers. Those times were scarce and happened before she left the military for good.

Walking behind her, he noted very few changes in the house. Although, since she garnered ninety-nine percent of his attention, he could've missed something. When she stepped into the living room, he followed closely behind, waiting for her to pick a place to sit.

A hand at the small of her back kept her from selecting the

armchair. Her attempt to put space between them was obvious. Rhine wasn't having it. Guiding her to the loveseat, he waited until she sat before sitting next to her.

Patience was a virtue Rhine could only apply in certain situations. This wasn't one of them. It felt as if seeing Vivienne earlier had flipped a switch inside him, and there was no way to turn it off. She looked everywhere but at him until he lightly gripped her chin, turning her face back toward his.

"Talk to me, Rose."

"No."

Not wanting to hurt her, Rhine released his hold on her face. His body was too tense to be trusted to hold her gently.

"No, you won't talk to me?"

Shaking her head, Vivienne's eyes darted away before meeting his again.

"No, I wouldn't have called if you hadn't seen me. At least not today."

Her admission was a gut punch from a prizefighter. No, not a punch. A kick from a horse. A big, muscular workhorse. It's a wonder he could still breathe—let alone form full sentences. Thankfully, all he needed were a couple of words.

"Why not?"

Vivienne tortured her bottom lip for a few beats before looking at him again.

"When I left—ended things, I thought that was it for us. It's been years. For all I knew, you'd met someone by now. Assuming you be available to me when I hit town was presumptuous."

"The hell it was. And we both know if I were with someone, word would've gotten back to you by now—especially with Roth and Autumn being engaged. Our families mingle together more than ever. One of them would've mentioned me having a woman on my arm."

"There was no way for me to know that, Rhine."

Lifting and lowering one shoulder, Vivienne took her eyes away from him, focusing on some point across the room. *Nope. That wouldn't do.* Crowding her in the already limited space, Rhine bracketed her body with his arms braced against the side and back of the small sofa.

"Notice how I didn't ask if you were seeing someone?"

Vivienne's thick lashes didn't hide the surprise in her eyes.

"That's because I didn't care, Rose. Any man who thinks you belong to him is in for a very rude awakening. And for the record, me respecting your wishes and staying away while you were in South Dakota doesn't mean shit. The second you knew you were coming home, you should've called me. Texted. Emailed. Something besides what you actually did, which was nothing."

Rhine didn't care how much it exposed him; he wanted to make himself one hundred percent clear to Vivienne DeNay Daley. With their proximity, closing her eyes was the only way for her to avoid direct eye contact. She didn't. Even though he was certain she wanted to have any conversation other than this one, she didn't close her eyes or try to hide from him.

"I'm not."

"You're not what, Rose?"

"I'm not seeing anyone."

"Good. One less ass to kick."

One corner of Vivienne's lips tilted up before she shut her face down again, shifting to something closer to neutral. But she wasn't quick enough. He'd seen it—the chink in her armor.

"You like that? The thought of me beating the shit out of someone for thinking he has the right to touch you?"

The shaking of Vivienne's head didn't match the banked heat he detected in her gaze. She liked it. When they were together before, they'd said no strings. But neither of them was with anyone other than each other. Rhine had no shame in knowing that to be true, just like he knew about the one time she'd gone on a date with an Ironhaven local. She saved that bastard a special visit when she didn't go out with him again.

With one hand at her nape, he used his thumb to tilt her chin, offering him a better angle to press his lips to hers. The encounter in his office seemed like eons ago the second his tongue tasted hers. Logically, he knew it wasn't possible to make up for lost time. It wouldn't stop Rhine from giving in to the urge to consume as much of his Rose as often as he could.

Swallowing her moan, he gathered her closer, until she straddled his lap again. Once she wound her hips in an inviting circle against his stiffening cock, Rhine stood. Still holding her in his arms, he strode from the living room. No instructions were necessary for him to locate the bedroom. The layout of the house was etched in his memory.

He set Vivienne on her feet long enough to strip her clothes from her body. Then, tossing the bedcovers back, he laid her on the sheets, spreading her thighs wide, offering him a perfect view of her delectable pussy. He must have stood there staring for too long, because she released a little huffing whimper before trying to close her legs.

Keeping them open with one hand on each thigh, Rhine's gaze remained on her puffy lips. She could say she didn't plan for them to hook up again, but she kept her pussy groomed just the way he liked it. Not completely hairless, but well-maintained, with a little tuft of hair right above the little hood hiding her clit.

"Stop it, Rose. Sweetie Pie and I have more to talk about. So, you just behave."

Rhine's rumbling moan drowned out whatever she said in response as he swiped her sweetness with his tongue. Giving Sweetie Pie an appreciative kiss, he flexed his fingers against

Vivienne's thighs in a silent command before switching his attention to coaxing her pearl out to play.

One, then two fingers slid into her slickness, flicking in a come-hither motion, causing her hips to buck upward into his mouth. She could crack his damn jaw for all Rhine cared. He wasn't stopping until Sweetie Pie blessed him with her cream.

"Rhine..."

His name was a whine on Vivienne's lips, and her fingers found their way into his hair, tugging at his short locks. The light sting was incentive. Using his shoulders to hold her legs open, Rhine reached up her torso, filling his hand with one of her bountiful breasts. It turned him on when she touched herself, but he prided himself on being able to get her there without an assist.

Once he tweaked her nipple while sucking her clit and strumming her walls, he got what he wanted. Vivienne's body locked, her thighs pressed against his shoulders, attempting to close, and a keening wail rang out into the room.

"Fuck! Hart!!"

That's what he was looking for—the moment when she let go. Lapping up his prize, Rhine ignored his dick's demands. He wouldn't waste a drop of her sweet essence. He'd earned it. When she was just a puddle of shivers, he finally released his hold. Standing, he shucked off his clothes without regard for where they landed.

The second he was naked, he covered her body with his, kissing his way from her navel to her lips, sharing her taste with her. Her eyes were closed, but she wasn't sleeping. Opening her mouth, she licked at his lips, tangling her tongue with his. The blunt tips of her nails dug into his sides. Her hips moved in an undulating motion—as much as his weight on her would allow.

"Hart...Please..."

Rhinehart's cock hardened to granite. Hearing her beg for

it. For him. It was the best aphrodisiac. Placing a parting peck on her lips, Rhinehart rose to his knees with her legs draped over his thighs, Sweetie Pie once again on full display. One hand wrapped around his length stroking from base to tip as he stared at his treasure.

"Please what, Rose?"

It was absolutely a dick move to hold himself so close to her slick walls but not enter. Instead, he rubbed the tip against her lower lips, teasing. Vivienne gave the bedsheets hell, grabbing two fistfuls when she couldn't reach his hips to pull him into where she wanted him.

Leaning forward to give her better access, Rhine dipped inside her walls. It was a shallow thrust that didn't completely engulf the head. Then he pulled back. A screech of frustration accompanied Vivienne's glare. Grinning, Rhine did it again.

"Please what, Rose? Use your words, darlin'."

Rhine barely understood her words when she released them in a quick, jumbled huff.

"Please fuck me. Please, Hart."

"When you beg so pretty, how can I deny you?"

Surging inside, Rhine buried half his length in her slick channel before backing out, then immediately thrusting again. This time, her velvet walls accepted more than half his length. It took a few more tries before he buried himself to the hilt. Nipping the space where her neck met her shoulder, Rhine kissed just below Vivienne's ear.

"Fuck, you feel amazing, Rose. Sweetie Pie is taking me so well. You should be proud."

Time didn't matter as Rhine stroked inside her honeyed haven, determined to get them both to the pleasurable peak together. As he moved, he continued to lavish her with praise, telling her how beautiful she was. How well they fit together. How hard she made him all the fucking time.

It was when he flipped her onto her knees with her

luscious ass turned up to him that Rhine stopped talking. Instead, he let his actions speak for him. With a rounded cheek in each hand, he lined up and entered Sweetie Pie in one swift thrust. Mesmerized by her jiggling ass, he pulled out and did it again.

At this rate, he wouldn't last much longer, but Rhine didn't care. The way Vivienne's walls gripped his length while her essence coated his dick said she was right there with him. Even if they hadn't, her heaving breaths and moans of his name told him.

Dropping over her, with his chest pressed to her back, Rhine swept her hair to the side, kissing her nape.

"Come for me, Rose. Cover me with your sweet juices. Show me how good I make you feel."

As if he'd discovered the Rosetta Stone to decoding her orgasm, Vivienne's walls tightened around his length so much he could barely move inside her. The heat. The snugness of the fit. Her keening sighs. It was all too much for Rhine to hold on any longer.

With a jerking grunt, he released his hold on his own orgasm, flooding her channel with his cum. Not for a second did he regret going bare inside her. If he had anything to say about it, they'd never go back to having a barrier between them. No barriers of any kind would separate them. Not anymore.

# Chapter Eight

She'd done it again. Vivienne had let her hormones get her fucked by Rhinehart Stephens. And while her body had no complaints, her inner drill sergeant was using some creative language to tell her she wasn't very bright.

If she had been smart, she would've talked to Rhine in her driveway. She wouldn't have let him in her house, and she definitely would've stopped him from taking his big-ass boots off and putting them beside hers on the rack. All of that was a recipe for trouble, and she walked right into it like she didn't see it coming.

Although she'd expected him to press her more to talk about them, and why she was so set on them not seeing each other while she was away, when he didn't do it, she was relieved. If she were honest with herself, she welcomed the distraction of sex, even if this time his praise sounded different. The things he said sounded...permanent. Not at all like their interludes over the years.

After he nearly fucked her to sleep, Rhine ran them a bath. When she was building the house, she'd insisted on the big jetted bathtub. Yet, she rarely used it before she left for

Ironhaven. But it didn't surprise her when he located bath salts to drop into the water or something to make fragrant bubbles.

Once they settled inside, she sat between his legs with her back resting against him. Vivienne was so relaxed she might have been willing to try talking—maybe really answer his questions instead of deflecting. But Rhine surprised her.

Running one thick finger along her shoulder, then down her arm, he didn't stop until he reached her wrist, where he reversed course, stopping at the underside of her chin.

"I know you aren't ready to talk to me about it, Baby. So, for now, I'll wait."

Holding her chin between his thumb and forefinger, he tilted her head until their eyes met.

"But my patience doesn't extend to us going back to the way things were. I won't settle for a piece of you, Rose, because I have no intention of only giving you part of me."

Vivienne's trapped breath refused to move past her throat, and her heartbeat was a drum pounding in her ears. Was he saying what it sounded like he was saying? The two of them. Together. In the open. As an actual couple? Could she do that with him?

The kiss Rhine placed on her lips was firm. Possessive. And completely consuming.

"Those are my terms, Rose. And they're non-negotiable."

If Trent, or one of her other friends, had come to Vivienne and told her a man pitched a relationship to them like this, she would've laughed her ass off. But this man had really looked her in the face and essentially said, 'You're going to be with me, or we're going to be together.' And from this side of things, that shit wasn't so funny.

"Breathe, Baby. The only time I want you fainting is from pleasure, and I don't think Sweetie Pie can take another round today for me to demonstrate."

Speechless, all Vivienne could do was shake her head. Rhine's broad smile transformed his entire face, making her forget he'd just dropped a batshit crazy ultimatum in her lap. Then, as if he hadn't just demanded they be together, he started talking about plans for getting Sunset Ranch ready for the future she wanted to transition the place into.

No matter how off-the-wall he had sounded moments before, the things he said regarding planning and what she needed to consider in order to move her dream beyond the idea phase were sharp. The man knew all aspects of ranching life, from the business perspective to physical work with livestock. And since he shared her love of horses, he had great insights for them to get started with initial marketing ideas.

After their bath, they fell into bed. Sleep claimed Vivienne quickly, and morning came with Rhine kissing her awake to tell her goodbye. He had early meetings but finagled a promise from her to block off her afternoon for them to discuss their project.

When it had become *their project,* Vivienne couldn't say. But she didn't argue. Instead, she noted that the sun wasn't up yet; so, she could sleep for at least another hour. Rhine's whiskers tickled, making her release sleepy giggles before burying her face in the pillow to get away.

"Have a good day, Rose. See you this afternoon."

He didn't leave until he heard her mumbled reply. Once he was gone, sleep eluded her. His scent clinging to the sheets didn't help matters; so, Vivienne left the bed to get her day started.

She was sitting down for breakfast when her phone rang. Almost positive it was Rhine, she swiped to answer without checking the display.

"I'm up. I told you I have things to do today as well."

"I'm positive you told me no such thing, but now I'm

interested in knowing who you thought would be on the other end of this call."

Hearing the voice of her best friend, Vivienne dropped her fork, lightly smacking her forehead with her palm.

"Trent, why are you calling me with the chickens?"

"I'll have you know my bestie told me the chickens get up with the sun, and the sun has been up for at least an hour where you are."

Sucking her teeth, Vivienne picked up her fork, eyeing the cellphone screen with growing suspicion.

"You might be right, but you're an hour behind me. So, my statement holds. What's going on?"

Vivienne detected rustling in Trent's background before he spoke again.

"Nah-uh. You first."

Experience, borne from their more than a decade-long friendship, told Vivienne that Trent would wait her out. If she didn't give him something, she'd never find out what had her friend worked up enough to call her so early in the morning. They typically talked when he was driving into work, but that was still an hour away from the current time.

Suddenly, Vivienne's eggs and toast held a little less appeal. Looking at the fluffy yellow humps on the plate next to the lightly browned toast, Vivienne pushed it away, leaning her forearms on the table.

"Okay...fine." Biting her bottom lip, Vivienne gritted out her words. "I ran into Rhine yesterday and we kinda hooked up."

Spoken quickly and between her teeth, it was amazing Trent understood a single word, let alone an entire sentence. But her best friend was fluent in Vivi-speak.

"No. Absolutely not, ma'am. Don't you dare try your walk of shame word jumble on me."

Sitting up straight, Vivienne's brow dipped.

"I'll have you know there was no walk of shame."

Unless when she left Rhine's office counted. And Vivienne decided it didn't.

"Oh...so if you're so proud of what happened, why are you blurting stuff out like a teenager caught out after curfew?"

She really couldn't stand him. It was a wonder how they had managed to stay friends for the past thirteen years through deployments and assignments in different parts of the world. But they had. And Trent knew her better than anyone else, which was why he felt comfortable calling her on her shit.

"You know what, Trent? You asked. I told you. That's all I'm going to say about it right now. So, let's get to what has you up early. Spill it."

"You know Javier was up for a promotion to Master Sergeant, right?"

Vivienne's stomach dropped. The tone of Trent's voice was enough for her to know what happened before he spoke. In the many ways the military had become progressive, openly gay men still had obstacles to advancement.

That someone with Javi's service record, not to mention his highly decorated years of service, was not eligible for promotion from E-7 to E-8 was infuriating. So much so that Vivienne launched into a tirade about the commanding officers being idiots. She dug deep into her bag to pull out some gems she'd learned from her drill sergeant during basic.

"And another thing. If they can't appreciate him, they can all suck a bag of diseased dicks."

"Damn, Daley... Tell me how you really feel."

Her anger brought about the return of her appetite. Stabbing her cold eggs, Vivienne mumbled around them.

"I'm just sayin'."

Trent's chuckles were the only sound louder than Vivienne chomping on her toast. *Needs apple butter.* She didn't get up to grab a jar to add it, despite wanting it.

"Daley... That was...strangely sexy. You have a delightfully filthy mouth. Tell me again why we never got together?"

Stopping mid-chew, Vivienne swallowed her last bite.

"First of all, you're not into me like that. In case you forgot, I don't have a penis."

"You know there have been some incredible advances in medicine. They can give you a really nice penis now—a good one. Depending on your preference, over eight inches."

Shaking her head, Vivienne gave up on eating. Wiping her mouth, she placed her napkin on the table.

"You're forgetting one thing."

"What's that?"

"I like dick *inside* me, not attached to me."

Humor laced Trent's voice, making Vivienne smile, thinking she'd at least helped lift his spirits.

"Well, if you ever decide to switch things up, I think I might be able to talk Javier into becoming a throuple. He's always thought you were pretty. And you're already #Team-Dick. So, no need to convert you."

"Trent Holley-Flores, get off my phone."

Trent's laughter was the last thing Vivienne heard as she tapped the screen to end the call. Checking her watch, Vivienne saw she had another hour before her meeting with Clay.

Although she'd grown up visiting Sunset Ranch regularly and built her house on land adjacent to it, she still needed to hear about the state of it from someone involved with the day-to-day running of things. They'd already started to scale back, and Vivienne was hoping she could entice a few of the guys to stay on when the place transitioned.

Clay had been very helpful. Maybe he'd be one of them. It was almost guaranteed that Herb was going to retire and move near his daughter and grandchildren. Vivienne couldn't blame him, but his loss would be felt.

Just as she was walking out the door, she got a text.

Surprise lifted her eyebrows to her forehead when she saw who it was from. Kirk Gross.

> 605-555-1975: Hello, Vivienne. This is Kirk. I'm back in town, and I went by Silver Creek to see you. Andy said you'd quit. I was hoping we could go out. But I guess I missed my chance.

How the hell had he gotten this number? She'd only given him her internet phone number and had blocked him after their one failed date. Screwing up her face, Vivienne tapped the screen, blocking Kirk. Because whatever world he lived in, she wanted no part of it.

Shooting off a quick text, she contacted a friend on the ranch. She wanted to know how that creep got her number. Not waiting for an answer, she cleaned up after herself, put on her boots, then left the house. By the time she made it to the stable to put on Princess' saddle, the entire exchange had left her thoughts.

# Chapter Nine

RHINE STARED at the numbers on his computer screen. He was going over the most recent reports for livestock in the area and the state, looking at potential buyers for the herds currently on Sunset Ranch. He knew Roth had offered to take some of them on, but Rhine wanted contingencies for Vivienne to consider.

Looking at the head count of cattle, the variety, and where they were in their lifecycle, wasn't something he'd wanted to be actively involved in. It was why he'd gifted his portion of the Lazy Creek to Roth, making his brother the sole owner of the spread which had been in their family for generations.

But...for his Rose, Rhine dug into the knowledge being born into a ranching business had afforded him. Although Vivienne's family was into ranching as well, it hadn't been mandatory for her to participate in that life growing up—not the way it had been for him and his brothers. Of the three of them, only Roth really had a love for it. Rhine and Ryker did it more out of obligation.

So, they jumped at the opportunity to do something different the moment it was presented. Although Roth surprised them when he accepted a commission in the Army, everyone knew he'd eventually return home to the ranch. It was in his blood, just like caring for horses was in Vivienne's.

Her desire to use the tools that had helped her heal to help others was admirable. Rhine hadn't been told much about why she left the military shy of full retirement age. He wanted to know but hadn't pressed her when she'd shown up on his doorstep the first night she was back in town.

They'd come together like a house on fire. From the first time they had sex, their chemistry had been off the charts. They'd come a long way since they'd run into one another while she was attending AIT.

He'd experienced an unexpected jolt of concern when she'd explained that AIT was an acronym for Advanced Individual Training for combat medics. It sounded an awful lot like she'd be in situations close to actual conflict. That hadn't sat well with him. It still didn't, but at least Vivienne was no longer being placed in harm's way while caring for others.

This morning, he'd reluctantly left her in bed while he went home to get dressed to make it an early day at the office. Leaving her soft warmth had been a test of his will. Remarkably, he'd won this round. In order not to neglect his other work, Rhine had to make some adjustments to his normal schedule.

There was never a question that he'd help his Rose, and he had no regrets about the extra time it would require of him. Having her home in Lone Star Ridge was worth a few early mornings and late days.

Jotting down a few of the names he saw, Rhine noted which ones to look into further before bringing it up to Vivienne. Next on his list was becoming more familiar with the type of place she wanted to turn the Sunset into. He had a basic idea, but she'd have to fill in the blanks with specifics.

Rhine had informed her when he left of his intention for

them to meet during the afternoon. Pressing the intercom button, he waited for his assistant to answer. Although it was earlier than when many in the office arrived, he knew she'd be there.

"Yes, Rhinehart?"

"Claudette, could you make sure my afternoons are clear? I want to block off that time from now until I say otherwise. Any meetings will need to take place between the hours of eight a.m. and noon."

There was no hesitation in Claudette's response, and Rhine had confidence she'd do what was necessary to make it happen.

"I'll get started on that now. Anything in particular you want to put on the calendar for people requesting time?"

"No. Just show it as unavailable."

Rhine heard the telltale clicks of her fingernails on the keyboard as she answered.

"I'll get on it."

It's possible he wouldn't need to give their project such close attention for an extended period. However, since he couldn't be sure, the change was necessary. Once his workday officially started, he focused on his tasks. Each meeting received his full attention, and he gave each report its normal thorough level of review before sending out responses.

By the time lunch rolled around, he was satisfied with his progress. Leaving some items for Claudette to look into during the afternoon, Rhine left the office. He'd sent a quick message to Vivienne, learning she was still at Sunset Ranch. Opting to meet her there, he placed a to-go order at a local diner to pick up on his way out.

As he exited the parking structure, he noticed Autumn standing in front of the Daley Building. Although she didn't look distressed, he slowed his vehicle to a stop and lowered the window.

"Hey, Autumn. Everything okay?"

Autumn approached the passenger side wearing a bright smile.

"Hey, Rhine. Everything's fine. Just waiting for my mama. She insisted on picking me up for lunch today. She wants to go over some stuff for the wedding. I told her I could drive to her, but..."

Her voice trailed off with a wry grin. They both knew how stubborn people in their parents' generation could be. But they also tended to be perpetually early for everything.

"Are you sure nothing's wrong? I'd think she would've been here before you were ready to go."

Shaking her head, Autumn waved a hand dismissively.

"It's fine. She called. My dad waited until she was about to leave to have one of his emergencies."

Autumn put air quotes around the word "emergencies," and her lips twisted into another slanted grin.

"We all know his emergencies are just him being bored because his golf buddies canceled, and he had nothing else planned for the day. I'd bet money he'll be with her when they arrive."

Rhine nodded. Having established that his future sister-in-law was okay, he bid her goodbye and continued on. He was surprised she'd gotten Roth to agree to wait as long as he had for the wedding. If Rhine knew his brother, he'd suggested a quick ceremony with a larger reception at a later date.

And by larger, it probably meant adding some extended family to the guest list. Even before joining the military, Roth didn't like crowds. Afterward, he barely tolerated them. Rhine wasn't as averse to them. He could do with them or without them.

Although he wouldn't call himself extremely social, he did more mingling than his older brother. He considered it a hazard of the job. Once he took over as CEO of SI, he'd been obligated to represent the company at events, pressing palms with other heads of industry and politicians.

Since he usually learned something from other CEOs and CFOs, Rhine didn't mind it so much. The politicians he could do without. But many of his clients received government subsidies and grants. So, he had to play nice with elected officials to maintain the inside track on programs coming down the line.

While government funds for horse rescues and ranches were rare, he'd already put out some feelers on Vivienne's behalf. He also had a few donors in mind. Of course, he'd already looked at S.I. options for corporate sponsorships for her as well. He was certain The Daley Group was also an option.

They'd never overtly discussed finances, but Rhine had heard about the ridiculous stipulation Autumn's maternal grandparents had placed on her access to her trust fund. She and Vivienne had different maternal grandparents, but there was also a trust fund for the children set up by their fathers once they started The Daley 1group.

As far as he knew, the terms weren't the same. Rhine would bet even money Vivienne had never touched hers. It was likely she intended to sink whatever she had to into the ranch. Mentally, Rhine added another task to his list as he drove away.

With lunch for himself, Vivienne, and Miss Hattie, Rhine parked his truck next to Vivienne's in the driveway of the main house. This time, Miss Hattie wasn't standing on the front porch. However, she appeared in the doorway by the time he made it to the stairs.

"Two days in a row? I'm gonna start thinking things if you keep showing up like this, Rhinehart Stephens."

Stopping next to her, he kissed the cheek she turned up to him. Grinning, he gave her a wink.

"What if I want you to think things, Miss Hattie?"

Swatting at his arm, her cheeks lifted in a blush.

"Go on now with your slick talk."

Stepping past her, Rhine entered the house, heading directly to the kitchen. Trailing behind him, she gestured to the bags in his hand.

"What's that you've got there? Something wrong with my cooking? You bringing your own food over now?"

"No, ma'am." Stopping, he placed the food on the table. "Well, what I mean is, it's not just for me. I also brought something for you and Vivienne."

"Oh, so it's Vivienne again? I thought I heard you calling her 'Rose' last night."

When the heat crept into his face, Rhine couldn't believe he was actually blushing. He was a forty-two-year-old man. His woman's grandmother pointing out his use of a nickname shouldn't give him pink cheeks like some teenager. Thankfully, his beard hid part of it.

Rhine knew a segue into a deeper conversation when he heard it. So instead of commenting on her observation, he checked his watch.

"Do you happen to know when she'll be back in? I thought she'd be done by now."

Moving toward the cabinets, Miss Hattie pulled down real plates. There was no eating off paper allowed in her house. Rhine had learned that from Nick years ago.

"She and Clay went off on their horses just after breakfast. I expect they'll be back any minute now."

Taking the plates from her, Rhine helped her set the table. The process was an excellent distraction. Hearing the ranch hand's name in the same sentence as Vivienne's didn't sit well with him. Knowing she'd spent an entire career surrounded by men didn't stop Rhine from feeling uncomfortable with some man he didn't know being with her so much.

By the time he'd set the table and Miss Hattie had produced a pitcher of fresh lemonade, the sound of footsteps from the hallway reached them. Vivienne's shadow appeared before she stood in the doorway leading into the kitchen.

"Granny, we're back. Something smells goo—"

Vivienne's words halted when their eyes connected. Rhine glanced at her, then immediately looked over her shoulder at the man standing behind her. He didn't like the huge grin the other guy wore. Rhine most definitely didn't appreciate the direction of his gaze. Vivienne's ass.

Standing, Rhine reached her in long strides. Barely sparing the other man a glance, he grasped Vivienne's hand, tugged her close, then pressed a quick kiss on her lips.

"Afternoon, Rose. How was inspection?"

It was possessive as hell, but Rhine didn't give a shit. The ranch hand needed to be put on notice and learn to keep his damn eyes to himself before they were closed for him.

Vivienne's eyes narrowed as she stared up at Rhine. Not even mildly bothered by the fierceness of her expression, he stretched out his other hand to the man. As often as he'd been at Miss Hattie's over the past couple of years, he was surprised he wasn't more familiar with Clay. The ranch hand being around more since Vivienne's return increased Rhine's suspicions.

"I don't think we've formally met. I'm Rhinehart Stephens."

"Clay. Clay Turner."

"Clay, thank you for showing Vivienne around in Herb's absence. I'm sure he appreciates you stepping up."

Rhine's words were cordial enough, but he was positive they didn't match the knowing look he gave the other man. Clay had a firm grip, but Rhine's hand was bigger, and he eclipsed the other man in height by more than a few inches.

Quickly averting his eyes from Rhine's hard stare, Clay looked toward Miss Hattie, dipping his chin.

"Well... uh... I'm just gonna head back out, grab a bite, and check in with the other fellas."

Taking a step backward into the hallway, he nodded toward Vivienne.

"Let me know if you need anything else, Miss Vivi."

"Vivienne."

Rhine's correction was immediate. Clay's head jerked slightly, and Rhine ignored the jab into his ribcage from Vivienne.

"Miss Vivienne. Miss Hattie. Y'all have a good day."

Quickly making his exit, Clay avoided any further eye contact with Rhine. A pinch to his side brought Rhine's gaze back to Vivienne.

"Seriously, Rhine? Are you trying to run off one of the best hands on the ranch? I almost had him convinced to stay on. Do you know how hard it is to persuade someone to make a career change after spending years doing something?"

Since it seemed she tried to keep her voice low, Rhine matched her tone.

"Is part of his agreeing to stay on here dependent on access to you? Because, he couldn't keep his eyes off your ass, and I'm willing to bet that's not all he stared at while y'all were out there."

Thinking about the way she looked seated on a horse made Rhine consider following Clay to have a little 'talk.' The sight of her on horseback, with her thick thighs encased in tight jeans and her round ass perched prettily in a saddle, was a guaranteed dick hardener.

Huffing, Vivienne whirled around and went to the sink to wash her hands. Giving him another withering glance, she accepted the chair he pulled out for her, then struck up a conversation with her grandmother.

Chuckling under his breath, Rhine contented himself with eating his food and watching Vivienne interact with Miss Hattie. They had plenty of time to hash things out between themselves.

# Chapter Ten

AFTER THE SPECTACLE Rhine made with Clay, Vivienne met him either at his place or at hers going forward. She gave him another earful after they left her granny's house. However, she was positive it went in one ear and out the other. Unsure of how to handle his new jealous streak, Vivienne opted for the path of least resistance.

Any other path required her to be a real grown-up and discuss her feelings. Negative. Abort mission. She could only handle so much, and delving into the layers of her feelings surrounding Rhinehart Stephens tipped her scales toward stress. Stress led to cracks, and the cracks invited the dreams. So... she gave him his way. She didn't push back on their meetings, which led to dates that regularly ended with them in bed.

Occasionally, they met at his office or drove out to the land. He wanted pictures to compare with the information currently on file from previous surveys. He recommended a new survey, and she agreed. She'd already been on the lookout for someone because she wanted to be fair to her other cousins.

While none of them were interested in ranching, they might decide to do as she'd done years ago and build a home on Daley land. Most of them lived in Houston. Only Vivienne, Autumn, and Nick had taken up residence in Lone Star Ridge.

Although Vivienne wasn't certain if Autumn and Nick counted. Autumn owned a condo outside Las Vegas before she moved back. She now lived with Roth; so, it was unlikely she'd want to claim a parcel of land to build on when she already had a home with her fiancé.

Nick built his house before Vivienne did. Stationed hours away, he wasn't there often. Taking all of that into consideration, she still wanted to give the others an opportunity. And in order to know what would work best for operations, she needed all the info. Of course, she'd have to run it all by Grandma Hattie before she could even pitch it to the others.

"Rose, I like this plan of yours, but I think trying to get it done so quickly isn't realistic."

Vivienne's stomach dropped. Once she'd really dove into the research of what it would take to convert the ranch, she knew it wasn't a short-duration project. It would definitely take more than the four and a half months she had left. However, hearing him say it hit a little harder. It made it real.

"I guess... I can talk to Granny. See if she'll give me more time. I mean, I'm here. She can see me working. She knows I have a plan. That has to count for something."

When Rhine moved his chair closer to hers at the conference table, Vivienne didn't resist him tugging her into his embrace. She needed the comfort of his arms around her.

"This plan...it's risky, Rhine. Not just for me, but for the hands already working the ranch. Some of them already have transferable skills, but the rest will need a lot of additional training. They may not be interested in doing so much just to stay."

With her head pressed against his chest, Rhine's deep voice rumbled beneath her ear.

"Rose, I'm sure your grandma will understand. Miss Hattie is a sharp lady. She knows businesses don't spring up overnight."

"I know, but the longer it takes to transition, the more time she's forced to keep things going over there. Although honestly, it seems like Herb and Clay pretty much run things. My dad and Uncle Travis step in occasionally. But beyond cooking for the hands sometimes, she mainly just signs off on the big things."

"Then she'll understand, Baby. Don't worry. As long as you can show her forward progress, I don't think she'll hold you to such a strict timeline."

There was nothing sexual about the kiss Rhine placed on her forehead. Yet, Vivienne found herself leaning into it. Into him. Lifting her face, she offered him her lips, and he immediately accepted. Pulling back before things got out of hand, and they made use of the couch again, Vivienne pushed against Rhine's chest until he released her.

"I think I need to go talk to her now. The sooner I can tell her what's happening, the better it'll be."

"If you think so."

Rhine stood with her, helping her gather her things before grabbing his own. As she pushed her laptop into her messenger bag, her phone buzzed with a notification. Thinking it might be one of the breeders she'd been talking to about horses for trail rides, Vivienne wasn't concerned when she didn't recognize the number. Swiping the screen, she answered.

"Hello?"

"So, this is your number. I was starting to think that guy was pulling one over on me."

Holding the phone away from her ear, Vivienne looked at

the caller information. The area code was 605, but it wasn't the number from before. It couldn't be since she'd blocked that one.

"Kirk?"

Vivienne couldn't seem to stifle the alarm and confusion in her voice. She didn't acknowledge Rhine going still at her mention of another man's name. He stopped packing his own messenger bag and stood up straight, staring at her.

"Yeah, it's me, stranger. Long time, no talk. I sent you some texts. Thought maybe I had the wrong number when you didn't respond."

"Kirk? Why are you calling me? How did you get this number?"

Apparently not happy with her questions, Rhine tapped her shoulder.

"Put it on speaker."

She probably should've ignored Rhine, but Kirk weirded Vivienne out. It's the only explanation for why she yielded to Rhine's demand. Once the call was on speakerphone, they both heard Kirk's overly confident voice.

"What do you mean? I told you I'd call when I got back from Europe. And I did. When I didn't hear from you, I stopped over at the ranch, and one of the guys said you'd left. I thought surely it was a mistake. You knew I'd be home."

"Kirk, I fail to see what you going back to Ironhaven has to do with me."

Vivienne held her hand up, placing it on Rhine's chest, silently requesting the opportunity to handle this herself. She hadn't been ambiguous when she told Kirk she didn't want to see him again. She thought she'd made it very clear.

"I told you the last time we saw each other that I wasn't interested in anything more with you. I was very clear that our one date would be our only date."

"Come on, darlin'. It's just me and you here. No need to play hard to get. You got me."

The obvious delusion in his response left Vivienne speechless. *Could he not hear her? Or could he only hear himself?* Rhine didn't have Vivienne's issue with verbalizing his thoughts.

"Do you need flashcards to help you see she doesn't want you? Don't call this number again. If you have any marbles rolling around in your head, rub them together and get a fucking clue. I'm only gonna say it once. Leave her alone, or you won't like how this ends. But me... I'll have a fucking ball."

Rhine smashed his finger against the end button so hard Vivienne almost dropped the phone. Swiping her finger across the screen, she blocked the new number. She hoped Kirk was smart enough to listen to Rhine and not call back.

Almost as soon as she finished blocking Kirk, the phone rang again. Before she could answer, Rhine swiped it from her hand.

"Hello."

There wasn't an ounce of friendliness in his greeting. Vivienne watched as his facial expression shifted from a scowl to a more neutral setting.

"Yes, just a moment."

Lowering the phone, he held it out to her.

"It's Canary Farms returning your call about the mares you were interested in."

Accepting the phone, Vivienne retook her seat at the conference table. Her conversation with the breeder was brief but informative. By the time it ended, she was ready to push the unpleasantness with Kirk to the side. Looking up to where Rhine stood next to the table, her lips stretched into a wide smile.

"They have three gentle mares they're willing to sell me. I just need to go look at them to decide."

"That's great, Rose. Did they say when?"

Nodding, Vivienne went back to packing her messenger bag.

"They said they're open every day, but the best time to stop in would be early in the week. Things tend to get busy on the weekends."

Having finished getting her things together, she stood. Rhine remained at the head of the table, watching her progress.

"I'll get Claudette to have the jet ready for us on Sunday evening. That way, we can go check them out first thing Monday morning."

Pausing in the act of pushing the empty chair to the table, Vivienne's gaze snapped to his.

"That's unnecessary, Rhine. I was thinking of driving, just in case I like the horses and we're able to come to an agreement. I could rent a trailer and bring them home with me. There's room in the stable."

"If you want to drive, we can. Or is this your way of saying I'm not invited?"

Vivienne hadn't considered that he'd want to go with her. After all, choosing the mounts wasn't exactly on the list of things she'd stated she needed help with. However, if he didn't go, who would help her? There's no way she could ask one of the other hands without Rhine having a complete come-apart.

"I didn't say you weren't invited. But you have a company to run. I don't expect you to drop everything anytime I need something. You have important responsibilities."

It seemed as if Rhine appeared in her space between blinks. With one arm wrapped around her back, he tilted her face up to his with a thumb under her chin.

"I know what my most important responsibilities are, Rose. Don't you worry about that."

Vivienne's heartbeat thundered in her ears. She wasn't certain they were having the same conversation. However, she didn't have the courage to call him out on it. Instead, she nodded, accepted his kiss and let him lead her from the office. They stopped at his assistant's desk, where he instructed her to get the jet ready; then they continued on to the parking garage.

# Chapter Eleven

RHINE WASN'T A HOTHEAD. At least, he hadn't been. Was he a direct man who didn't have problems speaking his mind? Yes. But did he routinely fly off the handle or blow things out of proportion? Until recently, he would've said no.

Yet, he was fuming. What he'd just witnessed, then participated in, was obviously harassment, or at least the beginning stages of a stalking situation, and Vivienne hadn't bothered to tell him a thing. He wondered if he hadn't been sitting right there when she took the call, if she would've said anything.

From what he overheard, the phone call wasn't this guy's first time trying to contact her. He said he'd texted. Vivienne not answering or even watching her block the idiot didn't bring Rhine any consolation.

Since he'd picked her up for lunch before they went back to his office to work, Vivienne sat in the passenger seat of his truck. She pointed her face toward the side window as if the passing landscape was the most interesting thing in the world.

In his preferred way to ride, Rhine had one hand on the steering wheel and the other on her thigh. Flexing his fingers, he gently squeezed her leg.

"Tell me something, Rose. How long has that asswipe been fucking with you?"

Her leg tensed beneath his palm before Vivienne sighed and turned to look at him.

"Was it weird that a guy I went out with once called me up out of the blue? Yes. But I wouldn't put it at the level of fucking with me, Rhine."

"You're forgetting I heard what he said to you. My hearing is *real good* too. And I heard him say he'd been texting you, but you didn't respond."

In his periphery, he noticed as Vivienne folded her arms beneath her breasts and pursed her lips. His hand remained on her leg, so he felt how tightly coiled her body was.

"I didn't respond because I blocked him. I never gave him that number. He only had the internet number I created. I don't know how he got my real one."

Turning off the highway onto the road leading to his house, Rhine nodded.

"A man you didn't give your real phone number to suddenly has it. He's been sending messages, and you've blocked him every time. Obviously, he's switching to different numbers because the block isn't sticking. Tell me again how he's not fucking with you?"

When he laid it out like that, Rhine got even more pissed. The urge to ball up his fist was so great, he removed his hand from her leg. The last thing he'd ever do is hurt her.

"What's his last name, Rose?"

Vivienne shifted sideways in her seat, staring at him. Tearing his gaze away from the road, he returned her stare for a beat before looking at the road again. He should've expected her pushback. It still ticked him off.

"Why?"

"Because I want to know his full name. That's why?"

"No."

"No?" He hazarded another glance at her. Her arms remained folded, and her entire body was tense.

"That's what I said. No. I'm not giving you his full name. You already threatened him. I don't think even Kirk is stupid enough to continue to pursue me when it's obvious there's a man in my life."

The little boost to Rhine's ego when she mentioned a man in her life wasn't enough to throw him off track. He wanted Kirk's last name. If she wouldn't give it to him, he'd find it another way. Still, he gave it one last try.

"Is there a particular reason you're protecting him?"

"I'm not protecting him. I don't give a shit about him. I'm protecting you."

Slowing down, Rhine made the last turn onto the long driveway leading to the two-story ranch home he'd built a few miles from his brother. The creek the ranch took its name from was a little over a hundred yards from his back door.

Once he was in the driveway, Rhine stopped the truck and put it in park. Tugging one of her arms free, he laced their fingers together.

"Rose, I know you're a badass with special skills and training. But you don't need to protect me. It's my job to protect you."

"Who says?"

Vivienne's eyes flashed with the flame he loved to see in them. Her fire and determination were part of what made her so attractive. Cradling the side of her face with his other hand, Rhine stroked his thumb along her cheek.

"Me, Baby. I say it's my job. And I don't intend to resign anytime soon."

Silence dropped between them in the truck's cab, but Rhine didn't attempt to pierce it. He just waited and watched the play of emotions crossing her beautiful face. Eventually, she squeezed his fingers and turned her head to kiss his palm.

"Fine. I'm still not giving you that idiot's last name."

With a brisk nod, Rhine closed the gap between them capturing her lips in a kiss. When her mouth opened beneath his, he almost allowed himself to forget they were parked near the road in his driveway. Digging deep, he found the strength to end the kiss, put the car in gear, and continue toward the house.

Despite his apparent agreement, Rhine fully intended to contact an investigator Ryker had mentioned to him before to get some information on this Kirk character, who couldn't seem to get it when a woman didn't want him.

Watching Vivienne sleep had become Rhine's favorite way to spend the early part of his morning. However, it wasn't morning. It was evening, and they were on his corporate jet flying to Robin's Corner in Kansas to look at horses.

Once he'd mapped out the trip, he vetoed any plans she had to drive there and back. If she liked the horses, and they came to an agreement on price, he promised to rent a truck and trailer to transport them to Lone Star. He'd originally offered to have them flown in, but Vivienne nixed that idea. She thought it would be too stressful for the animals.

The blanket slipped off her shoulder, and Rhine pulled it up, tucking it beneath her chin. Her soft sigh was reward enough. When they'd been doing the friends-with-benefits thing before, they rarely spent the entire night together. If they did, there wasn't much sleeping involved. So tender moments where he could watch her sleeping peacefully or ensure she was tucked in and warm...those didn't happen.

She slept so peacefully he didn't want to wake her. However, the flight attendant had just informed him they'd be landing soon. Rhine hadn't said a word to Vivienne about the things he'd noticed since they'd started having sleepovers.

Her sleep wasn't always as peaceful as it was on the flight. Those instances didn't occur every night, and when they did, most of the time, she didn't fully awaken. But some nights, she was fitful, tossing, turning, and mumbling things he couldn't make out. One thing he'd learned from his brother was never to wake a person in situations like that. So, he simply watched over her.

During those times, he was concerned about what she'd seen or experienced during her deployments. She still hadn't spoken to him about it—beyond saying it was a difficult time in her life. But, Rhine knew it had to be more than simply difficult if it disrupted her sleep.

### Two Weeks Ago

*"She has nightmares sometimes. I think she believes she doesn't have them anymore because she doesn't wake up."*

*Roth paused after lifting the saddle from his horse to look at Rhine. Nodding, he walked over to the rack and put it down. Grabbing brushes, he went back to his horse.*

*"Remember what I told you. Unless she's hurting herself or you, don't try to wake her. Even then, don't yell. Speak softly. Tell her where she is. Remind her she's safe. Repeat it a hundred times if you have to until she hears you."*

*Matching his brother's actions, Rhine removed his horse's saddle and began rubbing him down.*

*"She still won't tell me what happened. Only that her time on the ranch, working with the horses, helped her heal. Heal from what?"*

*Rhine glanced over to see his brother leaning against the wall separating the stalls with his arms draped across it. Roth's expression was unreadable, almost as if he was there but wasn't.*

*"Rhine, some things she may never tell you. You're going to have to be okay with that. I saw shit as a Ranger I never plan to*

*tell Autumn. As a combat medic, I can only imagine the things Vivienne saw while she was over there.*

*Being responsible for another person's life like that is a heavy burden. And no matter how good you are at your job, you're bound to lose someone. That kind of thing leaves more than a little mark on the psyche. Give her time. Don't press. If, or when, she's ready to talk about it, she will."*

*Nodding, Rhine refocused on caring for his horse. He knew Roth was right, but he didn't like there being something hurting Vivienne and nothing he could do about it.*

### Present

The plane touched down on the runway with barely a bounce. With one hand on her shoulder, Rhine rubbed in gentle circles.

"Rose, we're here. Time to wake up."

Raining soft kisses on her face, he repeated himself before pulling back. First one eye, then the other cracked open, leaving a confused-looking Vivienne staring at him.

"Hey, sleepyhead. We just landed. I would've carried you to the car and let you sleep, but I know you like to see where you're going."

That was a lesson Rhine learned the hard way. They'd driven to Houston to see an IMAX movie. She'd fallen asleep at the movie theater. Instead of waking her, he put her in the car and drove them back to his place. When she woke up in his bed, not knowing how she got there...it wasn't pretty.

Rhine scooped up the blanket that had fallen when Vivienne stretched. The action wasn't remotely chivalrous. It was the only way he kept himself from ogling her curves like a starving man seated in front of a succulent steak dinner. The way she arched her back pushed her breasts up, making them strain against the graphic t-shirt. Those talking robots had never looked sexier.

Thankfully, the flight attendant appeared to capture his

attention, informing him that their ride was waiting on the tarmac and their luggage was being placed in the trunk.

"Thank you, Felix."

Rhine looked at Vivienne's droopy eyes and decided to risk it. Scooping her into his arms, he carefully made his way from the plane. Once they were in the back seat of the SUV, Vivienne cuddled into his side. Her breath was warm and tempting against his neck.

"I can walk, you know."

"Sure you can, Baby. I just like carrying you around."

Vivienne offered no further complaints as she was in and out of sleep during the drive from the airstrip to the hotel. She was awake again while they made their way to the suite but was barely conscious when Rhine put her in the shower before tucking her into bed. Sliding in beside her, he wrapped one arm around her, being the big spoon. Although he wasn't sleepy, he watched over her until sleep claimed him as well.

# Chapter Twelve

THE ELDERLY COUPLE who ran Canary Farms seemed pleasant enough to Vivienne. Rhine walked silently at her side as they showed her to the paddock. The horses she'd only seen in pictures were grazing on the other side in a small cluster.

They were beautiful. Their coats gleamed in the early morning light, and they appeared to be a healthy weight for horses of their breed. There were two Tennessee Walkers and one American Quarter Horse. Their ears flicked with awareness as Vivienne and the others drew closer, but none of them spooked. That was a good sign.

She'd need horses with calm temperaments. If they spooked easily, it could be dangerous—especially for inexperienced riders. The Whitings had assured Vivienne these were three of their most docile horses. Since they planned to retire and had no children to whom they could leave the business, they were looking for suitable homes for the horses.

They mentioned offers for purchasing, but the buyers had only seemed interested in the stud horses and a small selection of the mares. Vivienne considered it criminal that anyone would look at these three beautiful creatures and not want to take care of them.

"The dark brown one with the white patch on her forehead is Petal. The one next to her with the black mane is Slim, and the one with the two socks is Ripple. They're all sweet girls."

Nodding at Mrs. Whiting's description, Vivienne continued to study the horses. She kept her eyes on them while directing her question to the Whitings' apparent spokesperson, Mrs. Whiting.

"How old are they?"

"Petal is five. She's the baby of the bunch. Slim and Ripple are both ten years old."

"They've all foaled?"

Vivienne doubted Petal had foaled yet, since she had just reached the age to be considered an adult. If she had, there should've been a colt somewhere around.

"Slim and Ripple have. Once we decided on re-homing some of them, we held off on breeding most of our mares during the last rotation."

Although she didn't say it, Vivienne thought it was not only smart but humane of them to consider what might happen to horses if they'd been bred and possibly separated not long after foaling and weaning. She watched a little while longer, asking more questions before finally getting to what she really wanted to do—interact with the horses.

"Is it okay if I go in? Make friends with them?"

Vivienne tapped the fanny pack around her waist. It held a few choice treats she occasionally used to reward or, sometimes, bribe horses.

"Absolutely. They're all friendly, and Petal never meets a stranger."

Rhine's hand at the small of her back drew her gaze. He'd been her silent support this entire time, but his touch halted her movements. Lifting a questioning eyebrow, Vivienne waited for him to speak.

"Be careful, Rose."

It was on the tip of her tongue to respond with, "I've got this,", but these horses didn't know her. And as docile as the Whitings said they were, it was still possible they wouldn't take to her. With a jerky dip of her chin, Vivienne ducked between the rails of the fence.

Taking slow, measured steps, she approached the horses in a wide arc. If Petal really didn't meet a stranger, then Vivienne hoped to make friends with her first to give herself the confidence boost of winning at least one of them over. Besides, she needed a closer look at all of them to be certain of their condition before she had a veterinarian check them out.

"Hey, pretty girls."

Time ceased to exist as Vivienne walked in a slow, wide circle near the horses but didn't approach Petal any further. Initially, all three lifted their heads, regarding her curiously. When she didn't come any closer to them, they resumed grazing.

Most of what Vivienne said to them was nonsense—compliments delivered in a soft voice designed to make them feel comfortable. Experience, combined with intuition allowed her to slowly gain their confidence. When Slim was the first to actually approach her, Vivienne wanted to break out in a celebratory dance.

Digging deep, she maintained her calm as the horse sniffed her, nudging Vivienne's arm with its nose.

"Hey, beautiful. How are you? I'm Vivienne. I came all this way just to see you and your sisters. What do you think about that?"

Sudden movements were a no-no. So, Vivienne took care when she finally reached out to stroke Slim's coat, giving the horse a gentle scratch between the eyes. Another nudge near the pack she wore around her waist made Vivienne giggle.

"I see someone is food-motivated. Okay, ma'am. Let's see what I have for you."

She'd already partially unzipped the fanny pack, making it easy to slip her fingers inside. Producing a carrot, she presented it to Slim, who nipped it immediately. Vivienne noticed how gentle the horse was despite its obvious eagerness to have a treat.

As it turned out, making friends with Slim was the ticket to gaining the trust of the other mares. Soon they all willingly stood still while Vivienne ran her hands along their flanks and inspected their hooves. They even let her look into their mouths without jerking away.

By the time she made her way back over to where Rhine stood with the Whitings, all three horses trailed behind her as if she held their reins. There were still other things she needed to see and consider, but they were off to a good start.

Rhine's arm around her waist felt natural as they made their way back toward their SUV. It had been a long day, and there was at least half of another ahead of them before she reached a final decision. The report from the veterinarian would be the deciding factor. She needed to see the records of their vaccinations and any illnesses they might have had.

No matter how much she liked them, Vivienne wouldn't introduce sick horses into an environment where they could infect other animals. Their normal vet would provide that information, and a vet of Vivienne's choosing would look them over as well. If she offended the Whitings or their vet with her preference for an outside opinion, neither of them mentioned it.

Seated in the rear of the SUV, Vivienne glanced at Rhine when he lifted their joined hands to his lips, kissing the back of hers.

"You were amazing today, Rose."

The blush creeping into Vivienne's cheeks surprised her. She'd received compliments on her abilities before, but hearing it from Rhine...it felt different.

She delivered her "thank you" in a breathy voice she barely recognized as her own. Staring at her with his multi-colored eyes, Rhine seemed to peer inside her being.

"Seriously, Baby. You're good. I always knew it. But seeing you work today was eye-opening. I can't wait for you to have access to horses that really need your sweet touch."

She thought the Army had effectively rid her of all semblance of modesty, but it seemed she was wrong. Vivienne wanted to burrow into Rhine's side to escape the praise he heaped on her. However, instead of shying away, she joined the praise party, turning the attention on him.

"What about you, Mr. Negotiator?"

Rhine had talked the Whitings into a better price than they had listed. It wasn't below the horses' value, but it was fair to the Whitings and, just as important, helped Vivienne's budget.

"Nah... It was easy once I realized part of their price was emotional attachment to the animals. When they understood you'd love on them just as much, they were willing to drop it to a more reasonable number."

"Well, I might not have picked up on that without you. I probably would still take them home with me, but I'd have eaten into my budget more to do it."

Vivienne scrunched her face at the tickling sensation Rhine's facial hair caused when he kissed her forehead.

"If I can't negotiate a good deal for my woman, what's the point of all those years in business school?"

Giggling, Vivienne tilted her face up toward his.

"What about the almost twenty years in boardrooms?"

A wry grin tilted Rhine's lips.

"That might've helped a little."

Rhine's heart beat in an even thud beneath where her hand lay on his chest. Unable to help herself, Vivienne stretched upward, kissing him, then swiping her tongue across his lips.

"Well, to whatever helped. Thank you. I appreciate it."

She'd barely finished her sentence before Rhine hauled her onto his lap, her thighs straddling his hips. Gripping her butt in his large hands, Rhine's eyes sparkled with mischief.

"I can think of other ways for you to show your thanks, Rose."

Casting a glance over her shoulder, Vivienne saw the divider was still firmly in place between them and the driver.

"Rhine...we can't. Not here."

Her mouth said all the right things, but Vivienne's body was firmly #TeamRideRhine. Her hips tilted in his hold, rubbing her covered mons along his stiffening length. When he leaned in, nipping the column of her neck, Vivienne questioned her own reasoning. Rhine definitely wasn't helping.

"We can do whatever we want."

Kiss.

"Whenever we want."

Nip.

"Because we're grown."

Suck.

If he kept up the intensity of his attention to her neck, there would be indisputable evidence of their activities left behind. Only the car rolling to a stop, jostling them slightly in the seat, snapped her out of the haze. Pushing against his chest, Vivienne steeled herself against the appeal of his sexy grumbling.

"Let's go inside. There's more space in the hotel room."

When his fingers flexed against her ass, but the determined set of his jaw remained, Vivienne rubbed her fingers along his beard, lightly kissing his lips. Rolling her hips, grinding her covered pussy against his hardness, she peered at him from lowered lashes.

"You know how you like to spread my legs and have long talks with Sweetie Pie. We can't do that in this cramped back seat."

"I'm gonna do more than talk to Sweetie Pie."

The rumble of Rhine's voice made his declaration sound more like a growl. He moved them from the back seat of the SUV through the hotel lobby and into their suite so fast, everything around Vivienne was a blur. The blur was quickly replaced with stars as Rhine delivered on every promise spoken and unspoken—well into the night.

# Chapter Thirteen

IT TOOK SOME DOING, but Rhine convinced Vivienne to use a trusted equine transport service to haul the newest members of the Sunset Ranch family to Lone Star Ridge. Her study of the company and its drivers would impress members of the government intelligence community. At one point, he was positive she'd contacted a friend to have them run background checks on the two men assigned to the task.

She eventually relented. They'd stayed beyond the two days they originally planned to spend in Robin's Corner, Kansas. But Rhine didn't regret it. He worked on S.I. business remotely while she focused on the horses and getting them ready for their new home.

Rhine had always thought they'd be great as a couple. Having had this time together showed his original feelings were right. Before, it hadn't been interest in sowing his oats keeping him from pursuing more with Vivienne. It was knowing he would never ask her to choose him over her career, and it wasn't feasible for him to travel with her from base to base.

However, when she left the military for good, he'd

thought they had a chance. That is until she abruptly ended things and moved to South Dakota. He was understanding...then. Now, he knew there wasn't anything she could say or do to make him let her go.

Hell, he'd placed himself right in the center of dealing directly with ranch life because she needed him. He'd fully intended never to be involved with ranching beyond the high-level services his company provided. But...it was for Vivienne. There was only forward for them now.

Based on the way Nabors Equine Transporters liked to do things, it would take them two days to get the horses from Robin's Corner to Lone Star Ridge. While she waited, Vivienne prepared the stables for their newest occupants. Rhine caught up on the things he couldn't handle remotely.

His personal cellphone buzzing pulled Rhine away from the latest quarterly reports. Checking the screen, he saw the notification he'd been expecting. The man was punctual. Rhine was pleased to get the message while he was alone. If she'd seen it, Vivienne would've had choice words for him.

A couple of taps on the cellphone screen set the phone to ringing. Barely two seconds after they began, the call connected.

"*Hallo.*"

"Good morning, Mr. Jansen."

"You may call me Gregor."

Smiling at the man's formal speech while requesting to be addressed so informally, Rhine corrected himself.

"Okay then, Gregor. I got your message."

"You will also receive a package in four minutes. We can review it together if you would like. However, the information is clear and thorough."

Rhine had no doubt it would be. He'd contacted Gregor Jansen after speaking to Ryker about needing a competent and discreet investigator. Gregor was the only person his brother recommended.

"Thank you. I'll look it over and contact you if necessary."

"Good day, Mr. Stephens."

The line went silent before Rhine could reply. Shaking his head, he set the phone aside, then pressed the intercom to let Claudette know to bring in the package the moment it arrived. He'd no sooner refocused on the document in front of him than Claudette knocked on his door.

"Come in."

"Here's the package you asked for."

Placing the nondescript legal-sized envelope in his hand, his assistant stepped away from his desk.

"Thanks, Claudette. Please make sure I'm not disturbed for the rest of the day."

"I'll get on it."

Rhine waited until the door was closed behind her before he opened the package to look at the documents inside. In perusing the contents, he was impressed with the attention to detail, even if he didn't care for what he learned. In addition to photos, Gregor included the name of the ranch hand Kirk duped into giving him Vivienne's phone number.

Learning he was right should've felt better, but it didn't. He was now faced with the dilemma of how to handle it without his Rose being affected. Having any blowback on her was a non-starter.

With a couple of taps on his cellphone screen, he confirmed payment to Mr. Jansen along with a bonus for getting him the information in such a timely manner. Only a text of acknowledgement followed the payment receipt. Rhine expected nothing less. Gregor didn't strike him as a chatty guy.

The interoffice communication buzzed, pulling Rhine from his thoughts. After checking of the display, he pressed a button to answer the call.

"Yes, Claudette?"

"I know you said you didn't want to be disturbed, but—"

A familiar voice interrupted Claudette's explanation.

"Rhinehart Stephens, it's your mother."

Dropping his head, Rhine couldn't suppress a grin. He had no idea why she was there, but Virginia Stephens wasn't one to be denied.

"Come in, Mama. The door isn't locked."

Quickly, he shoved the contents of the envelope back inside and put it in his messenger bag. Just as he stood from behind the desk, his mother waltzed into his office as if she hadn't just bulldozed her way past his assistant. The brightness of her smile was an immediate cause for suspicion. Meeting her on the other side of his desk, Rhine hugged her, then kissed her cheek.

"Hey, Mama. This is a surprise."

Holding his arm out toward the sofa, he offered her a seat.

"Wanna sit?"

Tapping his shoulder, she shook her head.

"No, I won't be here long. I just stopped in before I met Autumn and Carla for lunch. I wanted to ask you for a favor."

Rhine's suspicions increased. His mother reserved face-to-face requests for when she wanted to be certain she got the desired response. *Shit.* He was about to be strong-armed into doing something. Rhine could feel it. When his mama looked at him with a bright smile, he knew he was toast.

"The ladies and I are having our annual charity event. Each person was asked to provide an expert to participate. We're calling it Bid for Brilliance. Isn't that just adorable?"

*No.*

No, it wasn't adorable. But there was no way in hell Rhine would say so to his mother.

"Sounds interesting, Mama. What's it got to do with me?"

Knowing what she'd say didn't stop Rhine from hoping he was wrong. Swatting at his arm, she pursed her lips.

"Don't play coy with me, Rhinehart Stephens. You know I want you to be my expert. I'm sure there are plenty of people who would love to pick the brain of the CEO of a successful business for one day."

Part of Rhine was relieved that at least it wasn't some meat auction and he didn't have to parade around trying to get horny women to bid on him. But, something told him there was a catch.

"What's the catch, Mama? It can't be as simple as me making myself available for a day to be some kind of mentor to the highest bidder."

His mother's gaze darted away from his. After a second, she looked up at him through her lashes. He knew before she said anything he was going to agree. *Damn mama's boy.*

"I promise, Rhine. It's just one day. I mean, you'll have to come to the event. And, you know, dress the part for the expertise you offer. Maybe instead of wearing jeans and a button-down, you can put on a suit like you used to when you worked out of the Houston office with your father."

And there it was. The catch. Rhine rarely wore suits anymore. He had a closet filled with them; however, he preferred his jeans, button-down shirt and boots. The atmosphere in the Lone Star office space was very relaxed compared to the Houston office. It was only during board meetings there that he pulled out a suit and tie, or when he had to attend some type of corporate function.

"Mama..."

"It's just for a few hours, Rhine. You can sacrifice a few hours in a suit for your mother, can't you?"

They both knew he would. There was no point in dragging it out.

"Fine, Mama. When is this thing?"

"It's in three weeks. I'll send all the information to you."

After accepting her enthusiastic hug, Rhine escorted his mother outside and across the street to meet with Autumn and her mother. Along the way, he learned the three had a lunch date to discuss the ever-growing plans for Roth and Autumn's wedding. It was two months out, and his mother grew more excited by the day.

"You know I can't believe your brother is willing to have the wedding out on the ranch. I would've thought I'd have to fight him tooth and nail to do such a thing, even though there are so many beautiful spots to have a ceremony. Your father and I were married there, you know."

"Yeah, Mama. I know."

Rhine had heard the story of their wedding day many times. His mother retold the story, along with the pictures and video being pulled out annually on their parents' anniversary. Rhine didn't tell her the reason Roth was okay with having the wedding on the ranch was because it's what Autumn wanted. If he recalled correctly, she actually wanted to have it near the creek separating the Lazy Creek from the Sunset.

By the time they reached Autumn and Mrs. Daley, his mother had made it to the part where Rhine's cousin, who was supposed to be the ring bearer, laid down on her dress and fell asleep during the ceremony. Thankfully, she cut off the story, giving him a pat on the arm and a kiss on the cheek.

"Good afternoon, ladies! Who's ready to tackle seating arrangements?"

A smile tugged at Rhine's lips. From the expression on Autumn's face, she'd rather get a root canal. Seizing the opportunity to make his exit, Rhine stepped back toward the road.

"You ladies seem to have an eventful afternoon planned. I'm just gonna leave you to it."

"You're welcome to join us for lunch, Rhine."

Autumn's smile was a little too bright for Rhine's liking. Shaking his head, he took another step away.

"Thanks for the invite, but I told Rose I'd meet her at the Sunset for lunch; her horses are arriving today."

"Rose?"

Mrs. Daley's face scrunched in confusion. Autumn seemed eager to supply an answer to clear things up.

"Oh, that's what he calls Vivi, Mama."

"But her middle name is DeNay, not Rose."

"He knows that, Mama."

Rhine wasn't the least bit embarrassed, but the cute little flush of embarrassment in Mrs. Daley's cheeks, once what Autumn said became clear, amused him.

"Oh... Well, maybe another time. You have a good afternoon."

"Yes, son. Have a good afternoon. Tell Vivi I said hello, and I look forward to seeing you two at Sunday dinner."

The glint in his mother's eyes said it was in Rhine's best interest not to bring up the fact that this was the first she'd mentioned them attending Sunday dinner. With a nod, he quickly made his retreat.

# Chapter Fourteen

VIVIENNE LOOKED around at the newly erected addition to the stables. It was amazing the amount of progress the crew Rhine sent over had been able to accomplish. She recognized that some of the materials were prefabricated, but the structure was much sturdier than she expected. She'd been surprised to learn they were designed to withstand hurricane winds up to a Category 2.

Her belly fluttered at the thought of the day's events. She'd held off on talking to her granny about extending the deadline for the transition. Vivienne wanted to have something to show that she was actively working—other than walking around with a computer and meeting with Rhine in his office.

She wanted Grandma Hattie to see the changes she'd already made. Vivienne knew progress needed to be demonstrated before she asked for more time. The past week had been instrumental, but today was a big day. The horses she'd purchased, the first of the ones she'd need, were set to arrive shortly after lunch.

Her plan to turn the ranch into a therapeutic place was primary, but the trail rides were part of supplementing those activities. She had some connections for donors to sponsor horses and people, but training costs money. Anyone working on the ranch would require specialized training and certification, not to mention the necessary insurance.

Rhine had helped her wade through all of it, and it was good that he had. Aside from the training, she hadn't known where to start with coverage beyond normal ranch liability. The Daley Group typically took care of personal insurance for the hands, so Vivienne got them working on the changes in coverage.

"You look like you're about to hop out of your skin from excitement."

Vivienne glanced to her right to see Clay leaning against the top rail of the corral, smiling at her.

Returning his smile, Vivienne touched the tip of her hat, putting her eyes back on the dusty circle, wondering if she should walk it again to make certain nothing was there harmful to the horses.

"Am I that obvious?"

Chuckling, Clay held up his hand with his thumb and forefinger spaced slightly apart.

"Just a lil' bit."

Giving his shoulder a playful shove, Vivienne joined him in laughter. Music from her pocket interrupted their conversation. Tugging out her cellphone, Vivienne swiped the screen.

"Hey, Granny. What's up?"

"There's a truck with a horse trailer heading your way. They got a little turned around and ended up in my driveway. I sent them down there to you."

"Thank you, Granny. I appreciate it."

"No problem, Baby. That man of yours is with them. So, this time, they shouldn't get lost."

Vivienne's smile widened at hearing Rhine was already there. They were supposed to meet for lunch, then take delivery of the horses, but Nabors was a little ahead of schedule. Food could wait. She was eager to see her new babies.

Sliding the phone back into her pocket, she grinned up at Clay.

"They're coming!"

"Do you need me to grab any of the guys to help? There ought to be at least one or two of them nearby."

Shaking her head, Vivienne walked around the perimeter of the corral toward the gate.

"Naw, no need. There are only three of them, and they're really gentle."

By the time she'd opened the gate to the small holding area, the roar of truck engines was close enough for her to hear Rhine and the transport service coming down the road. It wasn't necessary for Clay to round up hands to help. The noise of the approaching vehicles brought a few of the guys out to see what was happening.

Vivienne's gaze was completely focused on the transport, so she didn't pay attention to the growing crowd. Once it came to a stop, she walked over to greet the drivers. The loud thump of a door closing captured her attention, and she saw Rhine.

It wasn't unusual for him not to wear a permanent smile, but his lowered brow and clenched jaw had Vivienne lifting a questioning brow as he approached.

"Hey, Rhine."

"Rose."

Not that she was expecting him to be overly affectionate in front of the guys, but his attitude was a bit puzzling. He barely made eye contact. His behavior was starkly different from when they'd parted ways after breakfast.

The Nabors' drivers stepped out, keeping her from investigating Rhine's issue. Following them to the doors, she heard the soft neighing of the horses inside.

Peering up at the high windows, she saw the tips of brown ears twitching. Her excitement grew by the second. She almost forgot to tug on her work gloves. Pointing toward the open gate, she spoke to the transporters.

"We're going to put them here in the corral first to get acclimated. I'm sure they're eager to walk around."

"Yes, ma'am. We stopped a few hours ago to let them stretch their legs, but I'm sure it was nothing like what they're used to. They're sweet animals, though. They haven't given us a bit of trouble."

Stepping up into the luxury trailer, the first horse Vivienne saw was Ripple. The Quarter Horse tossed her head a little as if in greeting, making Vivienne's smile even brighter.

"Good afternoon to you too, pretty girl. Are you ready to see your new home?"

Accepting the invitation to rub Ripple's forehead, Vivienne giggled when Petal and Slim became vocal.

"I didn't forget you two. You're both very pretty, and I'll be right there to give you some lovins."

Once Vivienne had said her hellos to all three horses, subtly checking their condition, they began the unloading process. Clay spoke as Vivienne walked by, guiding Ripple down the ramp.

"They are some beauties, aren't they?"

He stepped closer, holding out a hand for the lead rope.

"I can take her the rest of the way if you want."

In her periphery, Vivienne saw Rhine approaching. Quickly handing the rope over to Clay, she thanked him, moving to intercept Rhine. Stopping in front of him, she kept her voice low.

"What is your deal, Rhine?"

His gaze was glued to Clay for a few seconds before he made eye contact. She prayed he wasn't about to show his ass. They'd discussed this. Finally, he looked at her.

"I don't have a deal, Rose. I told you where I stand."

Getting closer to him, she placed one hand on his chest. "Rhine..."

They really didn't have time for this. Vivienne thought she'd made it abundantly clear that she wasn't interested in anyone else. Of course, there were always men who couldn't take a hint, but she didn't think Clay was one of those kinds of guys. Rhine's eyes lifted from hers. Following his gaze, she saw the driver leading Slim down the ramp. Tapping her hip, he set her aside.

"We'll talk later, Rose."

It was probably best they didn't speak about it now. So, instead of arguing, Vivienne followed him toward the trailer. He took hold of Slim's lead rope while Vivienne entered the trailer to get Petal. The other transporter was there, making it easier for Vivienne to guide the youngest horse from the trailer.

She was just about to open the gate to release Petal from her holding area when all hell broke loose. Yells and the pounding of hooves followed the high-pitched braying of a horse.

Making sure the latch was still in place, Vivienne bolted from the trailer. When her feet hit solid ground, she swung her gaze toward the corral. Her heart lodged in her throat while her eyes tried to make sense of what she saw.

Rhine was on the ground; his body was partially curled in a fetal position, using his hands and arms to protect his head. Above him, Slim's hooves struck out in the air. Vivienne thought her heart would burst when the horse came down, striking Rhine.

*God, no. No!*

The blood thundering in her veins drowned out any other sound as Vivienne raced forward. At the entrance to the corral, muscle memory kicked in, and she slowed down. Blindly gesturing to the hand standing at the gate, she ordered him to close it. Two other hands were on either side of Slim, trying to calm her, while Clay held onto Ripple's harness and lead, keeping her calm.

Everything in Vivienne wanted to run to Rhine. She wanted to scream at the other hands to pull him away from danger. When he rolled on his own, she couldn't feel relieved because his actions seemed to make things worse. If they didn't get a handle on the horse soon, Slim was going to trample him, doing serious damage. Her hooves struck out again, hitting Rhine's back this time, and Vivienne nearly lost it.

Approaching slowly, Vivienne called out to the hands. They moved as if they had some rodeo experience, trying techniques to draw the horse away from Rhine, making themselves targets, but Slim wasn't taking the bait.

Keeping herself within the horse's line of sight, Vivienne slowly waved her arms. The hands caught on quickly, and they backed away.

Vivienne didn't know where she found the strength to keep her voice steady. But when she called out to Slim, it was soft—calming.

"Hey, pretty girl... What's wrong? Did something scare you?"

A spooked horse was a dangerous horse. The urgency to see about Rhine battled against Vivienne's knowledge. Her years as a medic in the army compelled her to look him over to assess his injuries. Before she could do that, she had to get the horse away from him.

If she had to repeat what she said to Slim, Vivienne wouldn't be able to do it. Everything she'd learned about horses from childhood through her therapy training was put into use. After what seemed like forever, she finally got Slim to walk away from where Rhine lay.

The horse joined her several feet away, allowing the hands to get to Rhine. As much as she wanted to go to him, Vivienne focused on guiding Slim farther away. Once she'd safely tethered the horse to a post, she retreated—slowly. After she'd put enough space between them to assure she wouldn't startle Slim, she broke out into a run.

Two ranch hands knelt near Rhine. Her heart made a command appearance in her throat when she noticed he wasn't moving. Looking over her shoulder, she made eye contact with Clay.

"Call 9-1-1. Tell them we have a man down."

Catching the eye of another hand, she sent him into the barn for the first aid kit.

The nearest hospital was almost twenty miles away. Until she looked at Rhine, she couldn't be sure if they had enough time to wait for someone to come out or if they needed to load him into a truck and take him themselves.

Skidding to a halt beside him, she shoved the hand out of the way. Rhine's face was slack, and there was blood in his hair. The dust on his clothes kept her from seeing the specific places where he'd been struck. But her priority was the head wound.

Muscle memory took over as she assessed his injuries. Without her stethoscope and other tools, she couldn't do much in the way of examination. It didn't stop her. Someone shoved a first-aid kit into her hands, and she was thankful Herb had listened to her when she'd made suggestions years ago for the things they should add to it.

Using the flashlight in the kit, she checked his eyes for pupil response. She couldn't feel relieved to have found it normal because she had to immediately shift her focus to his head wound. She knew from experience that the amount of blood present wasn't an accurate indicator of the severity of a head injury.

However, logic didn't control over Vivienne's thoughts. There was so much blood. The best she could do was secure it with the bandages from the kit. They were almost immediately soaked through, forcing her to make a decision.

"We can't wait for the ambulance. We've got to move him."

Vivienne's training took over as she instructed the men until they had a makeshift stretcher to get Rhine into the bed of his truck. It was the closest option and had a long enough area to hold him. Due to his size, it took four strong hands to get him up there.

It would've been easier to put him in the horse trailer, but the vehicle couldn't move as fast. And time was of the essence. As they drove away with Clay behind the wheel and a few of the guys in the extended cab to help unload, Vivienne called out to those who were left.

"Carlos, call my grandmother. Let her know what happened; she'll take care of the rest."

Vivienne still didn't have all the information. All she knew was that the man she loved lay unconscious on a makeshift stretcher. Carefully, she brushed her hand over the uninjured part of his head, then leaned closer. Tears kept her voice at a whispering croak.

"Rhinehart Stephens, you wake up. You wake up right now."

Not responding to her demand, Rhine's chest continued to rise and fall, but his eyes remained closed. The tears streamed down her face so hard and fast that the wind whipping past her couldn't dry them. Kissing Rhine's cheek, Vivienne gently laid her head on his shoulder.

"Please, Baby... Please wake up."

The longer Rhine remained unmoving, the more desperately Vivienne pleaded with him. By the time the truck rolled to a stop in front of the emergency entrance, they had to peel her off him. With all of her training stripped away, she was a ball of emotions. She didn't know who finally got her to release Rhine to allow the hospital staff to work.

The action snapped her out of her grief and tossed her into a space she'd become all too familiar with. It felt like she was standing outside herself. Robotically, she responded to the questions the hospital staff hurled at her—giving them her assessment of Rhine's injuries.

Her cotton-filled ears kept her from clearly hearing ranch hands telling the hospital staff what they'd witnessed. But she couldn't focus on their words. It sounded as if they were standing at the end of a long hallway whispering.

When she came back to herself, it was Roth who was holding her shoulders. Sitting in an unfamiliar chair, for a split second, her mind played a trick on her, making her think it was Rhine, but it quickly corrected itself.

"Vivi. Did you hear the doctor?"

Blinking, Vivienne stared up into Roth's face, then around the sterile hospital waiting area. *When had she gone inside? Where was Rhine?*

"Vivienne!"

The sharp bite of Roth's voice pulled her gaze back to him.

"Are you listening? Rhine is going to be fine. He's just a little banged up and has a concussion. But he's okay."

"He's okay?"

Latching onto those two words, Vivienne felt herself slowly returning to something resembling normal. She realized her mother was next to her when she began rubbing Vivienne's back in soothing circles.

"Yes, Vivi. He's okay. The doctor just let us know they're moving him to a room for observation. He can have visitors as soon as they get him settled."

She wasn't sure her legs would hold her, but Vivienne

stood when someone returned to give them Rhine's room number. By then, she noticed his parents were present along with her own. Autumn stood at Roth's side, holding his hand. Vivienne's mother snaked one arm around her waist while her father stood silently on her other side.

"Come on, Baby. Go see about your man."

Slow steps took her from the private waiting room, following the Stephens family. The ball of fear in Vivienne's stomach hadn't ebbed. It wasn't all-consuming like before, but it was still there. Until she saw Rhine and heard him speak, she wasn't sure the feeling would ever pass.

# Chapter Fifteen

Rhine had never lost a fight. Not one. Not even before he hit a growth spurt and put on some weight could anyone boast that they'd bested him. That was before today. However, in his defense, his opponent outweighed him by several hundred pounds and had hooves instead of fists. Oh, and he hadn't seen it coming.

Coming awake with a start, Rhine frowned, peering at the form standing at the foot of the bed. *Why the hell was he in a bed?*

"Good, you're awake. It's about damn time."

The gruff quality of his brother's voice matched the frown dipping his brow, which remained when Autumn placed her hand on his arm.

"Roth..."

"Shhh, Sugar. I can handle my little brother."

Rhine would've shaken his head at his grumpy older brother, but he felt like he was peering at the world through a woolen veil and didn't have full control.

When he tried to move, a hand on his shoulder, one much too small to actually hold him in place, did just that.

"Don't try to move too much, Baby. The doctor said you have three broken ribs."

With difficulty, Rhine turned his head toward the sound of Vivienne's voice. He hadn't realized she was there. Once he saw her, the events from earlier came flooding back.

When he'd escorted the horse transport to the stables for Vivienne to take delivery of her new horses, he should've expected to see that ranch hand hanging around his Rose. He was always around somewhere. Logically, Rhine knew she wasn't interested in the man and he wasn't in competition. However, seeing another man make eyes at his woman didn't sit well with him. At all.

Rhine being preoccupied and trying to get his shit together explained how he ended up taking a blow to the head from an otherwise docile horse. As he walked Slim through the gate into the corral, he got her almost to the center. He was just about to remove the lead from her harness when he saw something out of the corner of his eye.

Normally, Vivienne's gentle touch had a calming effect. However, the longer Rhine was awake, the clearer his vision became. Something was off. His Rose didn't look like herself.

"Mama and Pop stepped out for a bit. I'll let them know you're awake."

Turning his gaze back to his brother, Rhine gave the barest of nods.

"You wanna tell me what happened?"

Rhine wondered why he didn't already know.

"Vivi didn't tell you?"

"The guys said she was on the trailer. They couldn't tell me much either, other than what happened with Vivienne getting the horse under control and taking over to get you patched up and brought to the hospital. Do you remember?"

Rhine wanted to bring his hand to his head; it felt useless lying on the bed. There wasn't an IV in his arm, but there was some type of clear tape on the back of his hand with a short tube hanging out of it.

"Leave that alone; it's for them to give you medicine if you need it."

Shooting his brother a glare, Rhine glanced at Vivienne. Why wasn't she talking? Beyond telling him not to move too much, she hadn't said a word. If anyone was going to give him advice on medical shit, it should be the person who knew about medical shit, not his brother.

"Rose?"

Not speaking, Vivienne simply held onto the hand without the port. Rhine tightened his fingers around hers. Staring into her face, he noted the slight puffiness of her eyes and the pinkish tint. Her shirt differed from what he remembered, too.

The commotion from the doorway pulled his attention away from his silent woman. Carrying a drink holder, his father entered after holding the door for his mother.

"Oh! He's awake!"

Rushing to his side, his mother leaned in to kiss his cheek.

"Rhinehart Stephens, don't you dare scare me like that again! You gave me four new gray hairs."

Standing up straight, his mother smoothed the side of her hair back as if it was obvious which four gray hairs had miraculously appeared.

"Sorry, Ma. Didn't mean to scare you."

While not as dramatic, his father passed out what looked like coffee to Roth and Autumn before coming closer to the bed. He gave a few pats to Rhine's leg.

"Good to see you're up, Son."

"Thanks, Pop."

Drawn back to Vivienne, Rhine resumed his assessing stare. Like a dog with a bone, Roth brought up his original question. Tearing his gaze away from Vivienne, Rhine first looked at his brother, then his parents.

"Best I can figure, after I led the mare into the corral, something spooked her. Could've been the end of the rope trailed on the ground looked like a snake to her. I don't know for sure.

I didn't have a tight hold on her, because I was getting ready to take off the lead rope. Next thing I knew, she reared up on her hind legs. Before I could get out of the way, I caught a hoof to the head. When I went down, I tried to cover up and roll away, but I don't remember much else afterwards. Just waking up here."

His father nodded while patting Rhine's leg again.

"You did what you were supposed to do, son. Just like they taught you when you were bronc riding—roll away and keep your head covered. Better broken fingers than a broken noggin."

"How about a broken nothing, dear?"

"I didn't mean I wanted him to have broken bones, sweetheart."

Tuning out his parents' little tiff, Rhine returned his attention to Vivienne. While his parents had left little room for her to speak, her silence bothered him. The way she gripped his fingers...

"Excuse me, y'all. I appreciate you being here, but could you give me and Rose a few minutes alone?"

If anyone had an issue with his request, Rhine didn't hear it. His focus was on Vivienne. Sounds of feet shuffling and the door closing behind them seemed muffled to Rhine's ear. Vivienne remained his focus. Once he was sure they were alone, Rhine patted the sliver of unoccupied space next to him on the bed. It hurt like a bitch, but he tried to move over to give her more space.

"Sit, Baby."

His attempt to readjust seemed to snap her out of whatever had struck her silent.

"Don't, Rhine. Stop trying to move around."

"I want you next to me, Rose."

"You've got broken ribs, Baby. Stop."

Holding his hand, she propped her hip on the bed. It wasn't quite what he wanted, but it was better than her standing there.

"See, I'm sitting, okay?"

Closing his eyes for a beat, Rhine breathed through the pain. He'd had worse, but it had been a while.

"What's this damn port for if they aren't gonna give me pain meds?"

"They pushed some acetaminophen but couldn't give you anything stronger because of the concussion."

Opening his eyes, Rhine found hers waiting for his. Unshed tears filled them, almost obscuring the dark brown. Uncaring of the IV port, he wrapped his hand around her nape, tugging until he arranged her on his chest.

"Rhine, no. I'll hurt you."

"Shhh...You let me worry about my pain, Rose." Not releasing her, he stroked her hair, keeping her head pressed to him.

"Besides, it's my left side, not my right. You're not hurting me a bit."

They remained in that position for a few moments. Rhine didn't want to push. However, he felt Vivienne withdrawing into herself. It reminded him of the way she'd go quiet sometimes before she left for the Silver Creek Ranch. Tilting her face until he could look into her eyes again, he swiped at the tears.

"I never wanna push you, but I can tell you're hurting, Baby. Talk to me."

Rhine wasn't accustomed to begging. Hell, he'd never done it. Until today.

"Please, Rose. Talk to me. If these tears are for me, they aren't necessary. I'm gonna be fine. I've got it on good authority; I have an incredibly hard head."

The tiniest twitch of her lips preceded her attempt to avoid his stare again.

"Hey...The Vivienne Daley I know doesn't back down. So, what gives, Baby?"

He battled with himself to stop her from torturing her lower lip, flexing his fingers against her nape instead. Roth's words echoed in his head, but this was one time Rhine felt he needed to follow his gut. Vivienne needed a little push.

"Nothing you say to me will change the way I feel about you, Rose."

Releasing her bottom lip, she closed her fingers around the hand Rhine held against her face. Clearing her throat, she met his gaze.

"Today...when I saw you on the ground...the blood... I felt so helpless. Then we got you in the truck and you wouldn't wake up... and I couldn't do anything..."

New tears gathered in Vivienne's eyes. Catching them with his thumbs, Rhine swiped them away, kissed her forehead, then the tip of her nose, before pecking her lips.

"I'm okay, Baby. If I heard Roth right, I have you to thank for it. You used your skills, and you saved me."

Kissing her forehead again, Rhine peered into her teary eyes.

"*You* saved me, Rose."

Whether that was exactly the wrong thing to say or the right thing, Rhine couldn't be sure once Vivienne began to cry in earnest. Broken ribs be damned, he gathered her to his chest, holding her close, and letting her release the pain.

When her tears tapered off to intermittent sniffling, he

continued to hold her. Initially, her voice was so low he almost couldn't make out what she said.

"I was a good medic. At least I always thought I was a good medic. During my last deployment..."

Vivienne halted. To Rhine, her breathing sounded shaky, but he didn't press her to speak.

"I was used to patching people up, you know? Worst case, I got them ready for transport to better facilities in an allied nation. Then... one day they brought in these kids. I mean, they weren't actually kids, but they were only in their twenties. So young... So young, and there wasn't anything we could do for them.

Only one lasted long enough for transport. They were short one on the flight team; so, I volunteered. I thought...I thought if I could just get him to a better facility, the doctors there could help him. I just had to keep him stable."

Hearing Vivienne's pain, her feelings of inadequacy, Rhine's immediate thought was to assure her she'd done her best. As his mind spun, looking for the right words to give her, she continued.

"All I had to do was keep him stable. But he went into cardiac arrest. I worked on him for twenty-seven minutes and thirty-three seconds... The doc on base declared him dead five minutes after we brought him in from the transport. It wasn't the first time someone didn't make it. But he was just a kid. A twenty-year-old kid."

Her body went still under his touch. Rhine rubbed one hand along her back and side.

"I'm sorry they didn't make it, but you did everything you could, Rose."

"It wasn't enough. And every time I closed my eyes for weeks, months after, all I could see was that kid's face. I woke up paralyzed, unable to move because my body felt as helpless as my mind. I couldn't let it go. Move past it. When the time came, I didn't renew my contract. But when I came home...the feelings hitched a ride."

"Is that why you left? Went to South Dakota?"

Loss was inevitable. Rhine was certain Vivienne didn't need a reminder.

"Being there...it was what I needed. The therapist helped me work through my feelings. The horses gave me something to take care of; they were so helpless, frightened. I saw myself in them. And every time I took on a skittish, abused horse and nursed it into confidence, the fullness of its potential...it healed a part of me."

Vivienne's eyes flashed up to his, and he saw a lingering hint of her pain. God, he wished he could take it all away from her.

"Today, when you were lying there, not moving, I felt like I was back inside that transport. Except this time, so much more was on the line. I used everything I learned with the tools I had available to me, but you didn't wake up. I haven't felt so helpless since..."

Rhine hugged her tighter, trying to will what strength he had into her.

"I'm sorry to put you through that, Baby. If I'd been paying attention—"

"Don't, Rhine. You can't blame yourself. Horses get spooked. There was no way we could've predicted it. It's just one of those things."

Kissing her forehead again, Rhine nuzzled the side of her face.

"I'm gonna need you to remember your own words. You can't blame yourself either. All you can do is your best, Baby. And I know you do that every single time."

Rhine counted her tiny nod as a victory. If he had to keep reminding her, he would. In the meantime, he held her, doing what he could to let her know she had his support.

"I really shouldn't be lying on you like this."

"You really should just stop trying to get away from me, Rose. I let you go once. I'm not doing it again."

Bracing herself on one arm, Vivienne stared into his face with a crinkled brow.

"What does that mean? I'm not trying to get away from you. You have three broken ribs, Rhine. I shouldn't have to keep reminding you."

"I feel 'em, Baby. I know. If I need you to move, I'll say so. I'm fine."

Vivienne's gaze softened, matching the touch of her palm against Rhine's face.

"What did you mean about not letting me get away again?"

Peering into her eyes, Rhine searched them, finding only the purity of her question there.

"I mean, when you ended things. I thought of coming up to see you, maybe figure out a way to work things out between us despite the distance. But you were pretty clear you didn't want me to come. And it was hard as hell, but I respected your wishes."

Pressing his forehead to hers, Rhine closed his eyes for a beat before opening them. This close, he could see every slight color variation in her brown depths.

"I'm just saying. I can't let you go again, Baby. I won't."

The slight scrape of Vivienne's fingernails against his beard was soothing, making Rhine want to close his eyes again to revel in the sensation.

"I asked you to stay away, because I was really messed up, Rhine. I wasn't sleeping. I barely recognized myself. To have you see me that way... it's not what I wanted."

"Rose...Baby. I'm not some asshole who stops loving you just because you're sick."

Vivienne's sharp inhale alerted Rhine to what he'd said

before the words fully registered. But he wouldn't take them back.

"I love you, woman. Then and now. So, no going back. No running away. No hiding. We face things together. You hear me?"

He was probably holding on to her too tightly, but Rhine couldn't make his fingers loosen their grip.

"I hear you."

A tingling sensation followed the path of her fingertips on his face. Turning his head, he kissed her palm.

"Rhine?"

Rhine stared at her with a single lifted brow.

"I love you too."

Rhine's heart soared out of his chest. He hadn't intended to blurt out his feelings. After he did, he hadn't given thought to her reciprocating. But she had. And now all he wanted to do was show her just how much he loved her.

"Ow! Fuck!"

"Oh, Rhine! I told you to be careful."

Her trying to get him to behave like an actual patient while he assured her he was just fine was how the doctor and his family found them a few moments later. Once he finagled a commitment from the doctor to schedule his release in twenty-four hours, Rhine relaxed against the pillows Vivienne arranged behind his head.

# Chapter Sixteen

"LITTLE GIRL, if you don't get a move on, you're going to be late for the shindig tonight."

Vivienne cut her granny a side-eye glance.

"I'm not gonna be late, Granny. It's not like I have to get all dolled up. Aunt Carla said I'm supposed to dress to represent my profession. Since I'm no longer in the army, my uniform is jeans and a t-shirt. They should count themselves lucky I laid out a nice button-down."

Try as she might, Vivienne hadn't been able to avoid her aunt. So, she'd been sucked into participating in the charity program sponsored by the Ladies' Auxiliary. The only thing that made her feel better about doing it was knowing Rhine's mother had bulldogged him into it as well. Now, as long as some scheming heifer didn't bid on him thinking he offered more than professional expertise, Vivienne would be just fine.

"Hey! Granny!"

Vivienne jumped and danced away from the towel her grandma snapped in her direction.

"Get a move on. If they have to come looking for you, they

might try to get me to go again, and you know I'm not going anywhere and missing my show."

"Granny, you know that show is on a streaming service, right? You can watch it any time you want, not just when a new episode releases. You could've watched it at midnight or when you got up this morning."

Placing her hands on her hips, Grandma Hattie lifted a single eyebrow.

"Did I ask you to adjust my schedule? No, ma'am, I did not. Now go on. Git."

Sidestepping her granny, Vivienne hastened to leave the kitchen. At the last second, she dashed back in, planting a quick kiss on Grandma Hattie's cheek.

"Love you, Granny. See you later."

"Love you too, Baby, but I doubt I'll be seeing you later."

Pausing at the door, Vivienne shook her head and continued. Her granny was right; she had little time to dawdle. Ever since the incident of his nearly being trampled by Slim, she and Rhine had fallen into a routine. So, she'd get dressed at his place, which was farther from the main house than hers.

"I thought I was gonna have to come looking for you."

She'd barely stepped over the threshold. Tilting her head up, she accepted his kiss. When he pulled away, she was incapable of not devouring him with her eyes. Damn, *he cleaned up nicely.*

He hadn't donned the jacket to match his suit, but the swirling mosaic in the tie around his neck brought out the blue in his eyes. Rhine tamed his short locks with a little product, making his hair shine beneath the lighting in the foyer. Reaching up, she stroked his beard.

"Did you go to the barber?"

Grabbing her wrist, Rhine kissed the inside before doing the same to her palm.

"Why? Do you like it when I trim my beard like this? You think Sweetie Pie will be into it?"

Since she couldn't tug her finger free, she swatted him with her other hand.

"Stop fishing for compliments that I'm already giving you. I was just wondering, because I don't recall your lines being so sharp."

Rhine's fingers flexed against the small of her back, and one corner of his lips tilted upward.

"If you must know, I made an appointment with Flip last week. I went by earlier today."

Vivienne's cousin Tracey, nicknamed Flip, was a skilled barber. If Rhine's haircut and shave were any indication, Flip might've just stolen him from his regular guy.

Stiffening her arm when he tried to pull her closer, Vivienne shook her head.

"Nope. I'm dusty. If you don't want to change your suit, this is a bad idea."

Rhine's fingers flexed against the small of her back again. Vivienne danced out of his hold before he could overpower her. Backing away, she felt behind her for the stairs.

"Do not start with me, Rhinehart Stephens. Your mother and my aunt are not gonna hunt me down because I let you make us late."

"Come on, Rose. I know all kinds of ways to keep myself clean. Besides, who said I planned to do more than give you a lil' kiss?"

Finally connecting with the banister, Vivienne shook her head.

"Uh-uh. You can't be trusted. You just stay down here. I already have my clothes ironed and ready. I just need to jump in the shower."

Rhine took another step forward; Vivienne took two up the stairs.

"I'll wash your back for you."

"No, you will not. You will stay down here."

His looking lickable in combination with his smelling delicious was dangerous, and Vivienne was no dummy. She couldn't let him anywhere near her, with or without clothing on. Suddenly, she turned, dashing up the stairs.

Since he didn't expect it, she got a head start. The thundering of his steps on the stairs made her shift into high gear. When she slammed the bedroom door, the sound of his laughter came to her through the heavy wood.

"Fine, Rose. Shower alone. Just know there will be consequences for running from me."

Vivienne's lady bits tingled in anticipation of said punishment, but her inner drill sergeant talked that trick into calming down. *Almost.* She didn't lock the door behind her as she made her way through the walk-in closet. Swiping underwear from the drawers in the closet butler, she dashed into the ensuite bathroom. That door, she locked.

The jacket to match Rhine's suit hung on the dressing stand he rarely used, and his shoes rested on the small platform beneath it. So, she knew he'd need to get inside the closet to finish getting dressed.

Thankfully, she'd gone to the hairstylist to get braids installed, so she cut prep time down to under twenty minutes. Hugging her scalp in a skillful design, the braids hung between her shoulder blades, stopping just above her waist. Vivienne stood in the closet, looking at her reflection in the full-length mirror when Rhine strolled in.

"Damn, Rose. Tell me again why we can't just give donations?"

Warmth radiated from where Rhine's hands rested on her hips. He stood behind her, staring at her reflection in the glass. While he stared at her, her eyes were glued to him. The suit jacket and designer loafers turned her man into a different person. He looked like the best-wrapped present she couldn't wait to open. *Merry Christmas in September.* It wasn't a real thing, but looking at Rhine, Vivienne thought it should be.

Steeling herself against the very impure thoughts his nearness inspired, Vivienne finally shook her head. Placing her hands on his, she pried his fingers from her hips.

"If you're okay with your mama showing up on your doorstep or my aunt sending Nick after us for making her cry, we can totally just donate and not show up."

The man actually looked like he was considering it. Swatting his chest, Vivienne stepped around him, reaching for her boots. These weren't the ones she wore on the ranch. They were another custom pair she only wore on special occasions. The brown leather gleamed with a high shine, and the lighter tan of the threads in the intricate design stood out in stark contrast.

Tapping Rhine's ass, she left the closet.

"Come on, cowboy. We gave our word."

His growl should've been a warning, but Vivienne didn't heed it.

"Hey! Ow!"

Rhine's hand was there to rub the sting away from the swat he'd placed on her bottom. Of course, he couldn't leave it at a simple rub; he squeezed the rounded cheek before giving gentler taps.

"I'm the one who does the ass-smacking in this house, Rose."

Rolling her eyes, Vivienne didn't bother to argue. It wouldn't make a difference. Twenty minutes later, he parked his extended-cab pickup in the lot near the event venue.

"You know they have valet service tonight, right?"

"I do."

Rhine shut the engine and stepped out of the truck. Grabbing his suit jacket from the back seat and slipping it on, he picked up his hat, then rounded the front, opening Vivienne's door. With her hat dangling from the fingertips of one hand, she accepted his with the other. Vivienne stepped onto the running board and onto the asphalt of the parking lot.

"So...is there a particular reason you didn't want to use the valet?"

Placing his hat on, he shook his head.

"I'm not letting those milk-breath boys drive my truck. Besides..."

Vivienne looked up at Rhine when he paused. He stared at her while she straightened his tie. Once she was done, she traced the pattern with her fingertips.

"Besides, what?"

Taking her hand, he tucked it into the crook of his arm.

"How are we gonna make a quick getaway if we have to wait for them to bring the truck around to the valet stand?"

"Valid point."

Nodding, Vivienne dropped into silence. Smiling and greeting people as they got closer to the building, she ignored the curious stares. There was no big official announcement about the two of them being a couple, but most considered Rhine a catch—and not just in Lone Star Ridge. Too bad for the tight-lipped mamas that he made no secret about who he wanted. Vivienne Daley.

Her smile got a little brighter each time one of them gave her a sour once-over. She even tipped her hat with a grin, causing one woman to grab her daughter's arm and flounce away.

"I think you like poking people, Rose."

Looking up at him through her lashes, Vivienne pressed one hand to her chest.

"Me? Poking people? I have no idea what you mean."

"Sure, you don't."

Either they had more participation than what Autumn

had told Vivienne about the previous event, or they'd learned a lesson about timing, because minutes after they checked in with the designated person, they led her and Rhine to the reserved tables. Mrs. Stephens was there almost the second they sat down.

"Good, you two made it. And look at you, Vivi. If no one is interested in a consultation, they might just bid for the chance to be in your company for a day."

Squeezing Rhine's hand, Vivienne gave the barest shake of her head. Why in the world would his mother say that? Did she not know her son?

"That's sweet of you to say, Mrs. Stephens, but this isn't about a date."

Holding one of Rhine's hands between both of hers, she gave the back a pat.

"Besides, it'll be more than a little disrespectful for me to go out on a date with someone else."

"Not if the guy enjoys eating solid food." Rhine's deadpan delivery left little to the imagination.

"Rhinehart!"

His mother's scandalized swat to his arm received a stoic expression from her son. Vivienne quickly intervened to steer the conversation in a different direction. Relief flooded her when another member of the Ladies' Auxiliary stepped on stage to get the event started.

First up were a few local artisans. Once the bidding began, Vivienne relaxed, seeing that the premise of the event was being respected. However, the second Rhine stepped onto the stage, the atmosphere changed.

"Next, we have Mr. Rhinehart Stephens, CEO of Stephens Industries."

Light whistles followed his introduction. Vivienne's head whipped around after what she was certain was a catcall. *These bitches...*

"Mr. Stephens has graciously agreed to assist the lucky winner with a review of their business plan and an assessment of their marketing techniques, giving them the benefit of his vast expertise. We'll start the bidding at—"

"Ten thousand!"

The voice cutting across the woman on the mic came from the left side of the room. Quickly locating the source, Vivienne narrowed her eyes at the woman. Before the moderator could recover, Vivienne's arm shot up.

"Fifteen!"

The hell that bitch would think she could buy a date with Vivienne's man. They made it to thirty thousand when Vivienne stood up from her seat.

"Fifty thousand."

Staring daggers at the other woman, Vivienne dared her to say another word.

"We have a bid of fifty thousand dollars. Do I hear others? Going once. Going twice. Sold to the lovely lady at table six. Thank you for your generous donation."

Rhine made his way back to the table, but they didn't have time to speak before Vivienne had to take her place. Grabbing her hat, she placed it on, carefully arranging it over her braids.

# Chapter Seventeen

Rhine thought if he smiled any bigger, he'd split his face in two. When she stood from the table glaring at the woman bidding against her, the fire in Vivienne's eyes was sexy as fuck. If she didn't have to get on stage herself, he would've tossed her over his shoulder. He was definitely gonna have her sitting on his face before the night was over.

Retaking his seat, Rhine impatiently waited for the person on stage before Vivienne to finish so he could bid on his woman and they could go home. Since it was obvious some folks didn't understand this wasn't a dating auction, he planned to bid first and high to get this shit over with.

"Ladies and gentlemen, allow me to introduce you to Miss Vivienne Daley. An Army veteran with more than a decade of experience as a combat medic, Miss Daley is also a certified equine therapist. She's offering the lucky bidder a one-on-one evaluation of your horse, as well as drafting a plan for any needed assistance. These services typically range between—"

"Fifty thousand!"

The speech about Vivienne was very nice, but Rhine was over it. Not even the prospect of getting an earful from his mama for being rude could stop him from cutting the moderator off.

"Oh! Well, we have a bid from Mr. Rhinehart Stephens for fifty thousand. Are there any others?"

"Sixty thousand."

Standing, Rhine scanned the room. Although he'd only heard the voice once, he recognized it. *Son of a bitch*. Walking toward the front of the room, the man wore a smug grin. *Fuck this*.

"One ten!"

The audible gasps could've sucked the air from the room. Rhine stared at Kirk, waiting to see if he had deep enough pockets and the balls to continue bidding against him. Wearing a shit-eating grin, Kirk put up his hands.

"I know when I'm beat... I concede."

It took every ounce of control Rhine possessed not to smash Kirk's teeth down his throat when he turned his smile in Vivienne's direction. Stepping between them, Rhine used his superior bulk to block Vivienne from his view.

The moderator continued behind him, but Rhine kept his stare trained on Kirk Gross. The fucker had saved Rhine a trip by showing up. Kirk was going to wish he'd stayed in South Dakota. Soft warmth slid across Rhine's palm, and he wrapped his hand around Vivienne's.

"Go have a seat, Rose."

When she shook her head, he broke his stare down of Kirk to look at her.

"I think it's best if we settle up and leave, Rhine."

Vivienne held his hat in her other hand. She didn't look at Kirk until he said her name.

"Hey, Vivienne."

Vivienne gave no verbal reply. She simply looked at Kirk, then back up at Rhine.

"Rhine?"

"Let's go, Baby."

Keeping himself between Vivienne and Kirk, Rhine escorted her to the payment tables. Neither spoke. It was a good thing. Rhine was too pissed to talk. He wanted to get Vivienne out of there, and he hoped Kirk was dumb enough to follow them.

After reading the report from Gregor, Rhine should've known the asshole wouldn't give up. "No" wasn't something he was used to hearing. Vivienne not only had the audacity to say it; she'd moved to another state, robbing him of the chance to get in her face to 'change' her mind. According to the report, Kirk pulled the same routine with more than one of his previous girlfriends. But Vivienne wasn't his girlfriend. And she never would be.

As they walked out the door, Rhine shrugged off his jacket.

"Rhine...what are you doing?"

Not answering, Rhine passed the coat to Vivienne while he loosened his tie.

"Rhine, this is completely unnecessary. Let's just go. I'll file a report with the sheriff first thing Monday morning."

Holding up the tie for her to take, Rhine shook his head.

"You can still do that. I'm gonna do this."

It had only been a few weeks, so his ribs hadn't completely healed, but Rhine didn't care. Kirk's harassment would end. Tonight. The teenagers at the valet stand looked in their direction. Rhine held up a hand, stopping them from approaching.

"Y'all stay over there. We're good here."

Turning to face the door, the wait for Kirk to appear was brief. When he exited the double doors, with his face creased in a frown, Kirk's steps faltered once he saw Rhine standing there. Arms folded across his chest, Rhine stared at Kirk.

"What's all this? Afraid of a little competition, Stephens?"

"Is that what you call following a woman who refuses to

date you to another state? Because that's not competition. It's a delusional, pathetic stalker. And we don't like that shit around here."

Kirk glanced to the side where Vivienne stood, but Rhine commanded his attention.

"Don't look at her. Look at me. I guess you didn't have any marbles to rub together. Now, I'm gonna have to keep my word."

Rhine's last sentence sounded almost cheerful due to the smile on his face. He hadn't lied to Kirk on the phone. He would thoroughly enjoy kicking his ass. The flicker of understanding in Kirk's eyes wouldn't save him—especially not if he kept looking at Vivienne.

"Listen, Stephens... No harm, no foul, right? If she'd told me she was seeing someone, I would've backed off."

"What?!" Vivienne exclaimed. "I didn't have to tell you I was seeing someone. I told you I didn't want to date *you*. That's enough."

Her next words were mumbled, but Rhine caught them as she backed away.

"Misogynistic asshole, I hope he knocks all your damn teeth out."

*What his baby wants...* Rhine flexed his fingers.

"Whatever, you're not hot enough for all this trouble. I don't know why I even bothered."

The last word had barely left Kirk's mouth when Rhine's fist connected with his face. The satisfying crunch was enough to make Rhine smile, but he didn't take time to gloat. Stumbling back, Kirk held the side of his face, staring stupidly.

"You hit me! Over her?"

Answering with his fists, Rhine delivered a combination that made it impossible for Kirk to speak again. Far too soon, the asshole went down and wouldn't get back up. Lifting him by the front of his shirt, Rhine delivered two more punches, the second of which knocked Kirk unconscious.

It wasn't his best work, but Rhine thought Kirk's bloody face and missing teeth were enough of a message. Wiping his knuckles on Kirk's shirt, he dropped the other man onto the concrete.

A small crowd had gathered outside, but no one attempted to intervene. Standing up straight, Rhine concealed a wince. Glancing at the speechless boys at the valet stand, he tilted his head toward Kirk.

"He's probably gonna want his car when he wakes up."

Not sparing Kirk another glance, Rhine strode over to Vivienne. Taking his hat, he placed it on his head before draping his tie around his neck and throwing his jacket over his shoulder.

"Let's go home, Rose."

"Whatever you say, Hart."

Her sassy grin earned her a kiss and a promise.

"Your favorite seat is waiting for you."

Running her fingertips over his beard, her smile widened.

"Well, you know how much I enjoy riding."

Rhine checked the contents of the saddlebag once more. Ranger, the older of his twin Shire horses, stood quietly, waiting for Rhine to mount. Scout peeked his nose through the window on the corral side of the stable, drawing Rhine over to him. Scratching between Scout's eyes, Rhine dug into the nearby bin and fed him a treat.

"I haven't forgotten about you, boy. It's Ranger's turn to go for the long ride. I told the guys to take you outside to play today too. Okay?"

"So, that's who I am now? One of the guys?"

Rhine looked over his shoulder at Roth striding toward him. He stopped next to Ranger, giving him a rub and a pat before coming closer to Rhine.

"You are if you're the person who came to exercise Scout. When I asked if you could have someone take him out, I thought you'd get one of the hands to do it."

"The hands are here for the cattle. If you want your babies to get special treatment, take them over to the Sunset. I heard Vivienne has added on to the stables, and she's hired some damn fine horsemen."

Rhine's chest puffed with pride. Roth didn't hand out compliments easily. So, if he thought Vivienne made good choices with her hires, Roth was sincerely impressed.

"Are you saying you're gonna stop boarding my horses for me?" Patting Scout's side, he tugged at his harness. "Did you hear that, boy? Sounds like he's kicking you and your brother out."

Shooting him a glare, Roth attached a lead rope to Scout's harness, then flipped the latch to open the gate and release him as if Rhine weren't standing directly in front of the horse.

"What are you doing? You're taking him out now?"

"I'm gonna put him in the paddock with Big Tex. I'm not gonna interrupt your little date."

Shooting him the bird, Rhine didn't otherwise acknowledge Roth's comment. With another pat to Scout's flank as Roth led him past, Rhine walked back to Ranger. Gathering the reins, he swung up into the saddle.

"Later."

Roth's responding grunt was the only goodbye Rhine expected. So, he guided Ranger out of the gate toward the open field. The wind whipped lightly around him when they reached a more open area, and he gave Ranger his head. Once he saw the creek in the distance, Rhine retook control, slowing the horse to a light trot.

As he approached, he saw Vivienne was already there. Seated on a bench on the Daley side of the creek, she waved to him as he drew closer. For a second, he forgot how to exchange oxygen for carbon dioxide. In a simple pair of jeans and a fitted graphic t-shirt, she was nothing short of gorgeous.

Instead of using the bridge, Rhine guided Ranger through a shallow part of the creek. Ignoring the water splashing around him, wetting his pants and shirt, he made his way to her. Her smile widened.

"You couldn't go forty yards to the bridge?"

Swinging down from Ranger's back, he tugged her flush to him with one arm around her waist.

"No. That takes too long."

Her lips were a plump temptation he refused to ignore. Capturing them, he treated himself to a quick taste of her natural sweetness.

"Hey, Rose."

"Hey, Rhine."

Before he got carried away and forgot the mission, Rhine set her away from him, unloaded the saddlebags, then gave Ranger a smack on the rump to get him moving toward where Princess grazed in the field behind them.

"What's all this?"

Rhine glanced at Vivienne but continued with his task, laying out the light blanket on the grass a safe distance from the creek bank.

"What does it look like, Rose?"

Whipping his wet shirt off over his head, he tossed it in the grass, then sat down to pull off his boots.

"It's starting to look like a strip show without the sexy club music. Hold on."

A few seconds later, a thumping bassline hit Rhine's ears. He threw his head back in laughter when he saw Vivienne holding out her phone, rocking to the beat, and waving what looked like dollar bills in his direction.

His boots and hat hit the grass next to his shirt. Then, Rhine stood up, closing the distance between them. Lifting her hand, he looked at the money—five and ones.

"What? I don't rate at least a twenty?"

"You've gotta take off a lot more to get to the big bills, cowboy."

Snagging her around the waist, he held her body close to his. The blunt tips of her fingernails scraped against his chest, nearly making Rhine lose focus. Kissing the sweet spot where her neck and shoulder joined, he tugged her onto the blanket.

"Stop trying to take advantage of me while I'm doing something sweet, and get over here, woman."

"Fine, party pooper."

Vivienne's body relaxed in his embrace as he lowered them both onto the blanket. Kissing away her pout, Rhine pressed his forehead to hers.

"Don't worry, Baby. There's still gonna be a party."

He'd left the contents of the saddlebags off to the side of the blanket. Pulling the bundles closer, he revealed the bottle of wine along with a selection of light snacks.

"Oh...Rhine..."

Rhine leaned his face into the kiss Vivienne pressed to his cheek.

"This is so sweet, Baby. Thank you."

Turning his head, he initiated a deeper kiss.

"You're welcome, Rose."

Rhine was pleased to see the wine glasses had survived the journey. Partially filling them, he passed one to Vivienne. Although he had packed plates and prepared one for each of them, they ended up eating off one, feeding each other bites of meat, cheese, and the fancy crackers she liked. He enjoyed her leaning into his chest and relished having her close to him in quiet moments like this. He wanted it all the time, and he knew there was only one way to make it happen.

Gliding his fingers along her arm, Rhine tapped her wrist before reversing course back up to her shoulder, then repeating the process. Vivienne cuddled closer to him, placing a kiss on his bare chest.

"Baby, have you ever wondered why I call you Rose?"

Vivienne tilted her head back, staring at him with raised eyebrows.

"I guess, in the beginning, I thought it was kind of sweet. It's not a normal nickname, but I thought it was cute. It was our thing. So, when you didn't elaborate, I just let it go. However, if you're in the sharing mood...why do you?"

"Because..." Tapping the tip of her nose, he kissed it. "Roses are beautiful. Just like you."

Vivienne's cheeks lifted in an adorable blush.

"Besides their beauty, roses are versatile. Just like you. So versatile, they're used in lots of things, from fragrances to medicines."

Tracing a pattern on her arm, he continued.

"People can't think about roses without being reminded of the thorns. They think the thorns are there for protection. And they are. But they also help the roses climb, making it easier for them to scale and cover walls, reaching incredible heights."

A finger beneath Vivienne's chin kept her face tilted toward his, when she tried to lower it.

"With proper care, roses yield strikingly beautiful blooms and bear delicious fruit. In you, I see all of those qualities and more. That's why I call you Rose."

"Rhine..."

A sheen of tears glistened in Vivienne's eyes. Pressing his lips to her eyelids, then the tip of her nose, and finally, her lips, Rhine poured every ounce of his love into the kiss. Tugging her until she straddled his lap, he wrapped his arms around her, enjoying her bountiful curves pressed so tightly against him.

Their kiss ended in slow parting pecks. If he hadn't stopped, Rhine was certain the horses would get the show of their lives. Tears no longer filled Vivienne's eyes, but love shone brightly as she stared into his.

"I love you so much, Rhinehart Stephens."

"Oh yeah?"

Pulling the navy box from where he'd stashed it under the edge of the blanket, he flipped it open.

"Do you love me enough to marry me? Be my wife?"

Vivienne's gaze left his to look into the box. The tears returned, and she covered her mouth with both hands.

"I can't hear your answer if you hide behind your hands, Rose."

Lowering her hands, Vivienne launched herself at him. Allowing their momentum to topple him, Rhine looked up at her from his back. He continued to hold the ring up between them.

"Yes."

"Yes?"

"Yes."

One hand at her nape pulled Vivienne closer until their noses almost touched.

"Yes, what, Rose?"

"Yes, I'll marry you."

Rhine swallowed her confirmation in a kiss. Soon, the ring on her finger was the only thing she wore. He didn't know if the horses enjoyed the show, but Rhine had a hell of a time putting it on, making love to his fiancée until the sun was dangerously low in the sky.

# *Epilogue*

"Mmmm... Yes, Hart... Just like that, Baby."

Vivienne kept her praises and moans soft, but she couldn't be completely silent while her husband gave Sweetie Pie morning kisses. His hair, slightly longer now, was slick beneath her fingers as she gripped his head. Her husband didn't need the encouragement; Vivienne simply couldn't stop herself from touching him.

Her orgasm took her by surprise. Vivienne tilted her head backward, but Rhine muffled her scream with his hand over her mouth. Evil giver of pleasure that he was, he never stopped torturing her clit. As thoroughly as he licked her, he didn't miss a drop of her essence.

A herd of stallions pounded in her chest as she gasped for air. Rhine had removed his hand from her mouth and filled it with her breast, massaging the heavy globe. Vivienne trembled in the aftereffects of her release. Yet, her body wanted more.

Rhine positioned himself on his knees with her open legs draped over his thighs. Devouring him with her gaze, Vivienne appreciated her husband's massive frame. His chest heaved with each breath, drawing her gaze to his pectorals. There was no six pack—just a solidly built man whose genetics gifted him with thick muscles. Muscles she quite enjoyed rubbing and lying on.

Jutting from his pelvis was the work of art that was his dick. Vivienne's mouth watered as she watched him stroke his length. A shiny drop of pre-cum appeared at the head. Without conscious thought, her tongue peeked out, swiping across her lips.

"Nah-uh, Rose. I promise to let you kiss him, but not right now. It's time for his meeting with Sweetie Pie."

Strong hands lifted her legs as he leaned forward, sliding his length into her channel without any additional guidance from him. Vivienne's eyes slammed shut, and her teeth clamped down on her bottom lip at the delicious stretch.

"MMmm!!"

A nip on her chin made her release her lip. Immediately taking advantage, Rhine licked and sucked it into his mouth, soothing the sting of her bite. His tongue sliding inside her mouth mimicked the motion of his cock delving inside her.

With her legs pressed so closely to her chest, all she could do was accept the expert pipe her husband was laying. Releasing her mouth, he trailed kisses toward her ear, nuzzling the sensitive skin at the crook of her neck. A particularly sturdy thrust forced a startled gasp from Vivienne. An unintelligible jumble of words rushed out with her breath.

"What was that, Rose? I didn't understand you."

Oxygen was at a premium. Vivienne couldn't waste it on words, but Rhine wasn't inclined to give her a reprieve.

"Were you saying sorry? You've kept Sweetie Pie from me for three whole days. Were you trying to tell me how you were gonna make it up to me by coming all over my dick? Hm? You gonna show your thanks by ruining these sheets?"

Vivienne's husband had a filthy mouth. And she loved

every syllable. Yet, not a word fell from her lips. Thankfully, he didn't seem to need verbal acknowledgement. He continued to batter her senses with his words while administering sensual battering to her pussy.

Far sooner than should've been possible, Vivienne reached her second climax of the morning. This time, Rhine captured her scream with his mouth, kissing her through it, then adding his own grunting moans as he reached his own climax. Her channel tightened around his length as it jerked inside her, releasing his seed.

He remained on top of her as he lowered her legs, balancing himself on his elbows. Vivienne stared up into his mystery-colored eyes while stroking his hair away from his forehead. Just as he leaned in to kiss her again... Knock! Knock! Knock! Persistent little fists banged against their door.

"Mama! Daddy!"

"Please tell me you locked the door."

Pushing against his shoulder, Vivienne tried to move almost three hundred pounds of man to the side. Snagging her hand, Rhine kissed her palm.

"Of course I locked it, Rose. I'm no amateur."

The knocks came again.

"Mama! Daddy! I'm up! Time to go rodeo!"

Running her fingertips along his flank, Vivienne grinned at Rhine.

"You know he's not going to go away."

Verifying Vivienne's prediction, the door handle jiggled noisily. Knowing she couldn't physically move Rhine, Vivienne nudged him by gripping her thighs around his waist.

"Rose, are you trying to distract me while our son is right outside the door?"

"No, I'm trying to get you to move. It's your turn to deal with Wake-up Call."

Their son, Daley, earned his nickname honestly. Although

he'd slept through the night early in his infancy, he'd been an early riser from day one. And once he was awake, he wanted everyone in the house awake with him—starting with his parents.

"One of these days, I'm going to have a talk with him about interrupting my time with Sweetie Pie."

Pinching his side, Vivienne shook her head.

"You are *not* going to speak to our son about cock-blocking."

"Not today, Rose. I said, 'One of these days.' He's three years old. As far as he's concerned, we exist for his convenience."

Rhine's facial hair tickled as it lightly abraded her skin with his hurried kiss while he levered himself off the bed. Securing the covers over her body, Vivienne giggled as he struggled into his joggers, trying to snag another quick kiss before he went to the door.

Opening it just enough to go out, he bent down, scooping their three-year-old into his arms.

"Come on, Bud. Mama needs a few minutes. Let's go see what your sister is up to."

Vivienne's smile widened as she caught their son's next words before the door closed.

"Ya-Ya told me to get out."

The door muffled Rhine's reply. As much as her body wanted to snuggle under the covers, Vivienne tossed them aside. Although Rhine was capable of dealing with their children on his own, they had a big day ahead of them. It was the first time both of their children would take part in the Pee-wee rodeo.

Maya was in the barrel racing competition, and Dale would make his debut mutton busting—trying to stay on a sheep's back for as long as possible. Since they'd had both children on the backs of horses and ponies from the time they could walk, Vivienne expected each child to do well.

Two hours later, while Rhine parked the truck and trailer, Vivienne wrangled their children. They were good kids, but she'd had easier times with some of the more spirited horses brought to the ranch. But what did she expect with the parents her children had?

She finally had them standing beside their gear while Rhine unloaded Maya's pony, Flower.

"Mama, I'm gonna ride good."

"You sure are, Baby."

Looking down at her son, Vivienne wanted to pinch his still baby-plump cheeks but restrained herself. His little brow furrowed.

"I'm not a baby, Mama. I'm a cowboy!"

Consoling herself with a squeeze of his shoulder, Vivienne nodded solemnly.

"My apologies. I stand corrected, Cowboy."

Nodding his approval, Dale turned his attention to his sister.

"You gonna ride good too, Ya-ya."

Some days, Vivienne wondered if she had a five-year-old or a fifteen-year-old. Maya rolled her eyes skyward as if praying for strength, then looked at her younger brother.

"Yeah, I'm gonna ride good too."

By the time they'd found their seats, the fifteen-year-old had disappeared, and Vivienne had her five-year-old back. Given the time between the mutton busting part of the competition and barrel racing, they had a moment for the family to cheer Dale on before Vivienne had to take Maya to the designated area.

It seemed like all of their immediate family showed up to support Maya and Dale—including her children's first cousins. Ryker, Ensley, Roth, and Autumn were all there. Nick and his wife had also made the trip. Of course, Trent and Javier flew in, bringing their ten-month-old, who was asleep in a carrier attached to Trent's chest.

The entire section appeared to be reserved for the Stephens, Daleys, and their friends. Vivienne's heart felt full to bursting at the support being shown to her children. It was a pee-wee rodeo, so it wasn't as if they were competing for national or even state titles. Yet, they'd shown up.

"Look, Mama! It's almost Dale's turn."

With two years between them, Maya and Daley had the normal sibling squabbles, but Vivienne was proud she and Rhine were raising loving and supportive children. Maya bounced on the balls of her feet, clapping for her little brother.

Standing in line with the other kids in his age group, Daley was taller than everyone his age and a few of the older children. Although Vivienne was above average height for a woman, she blamed Rhine for her super-sized children. Both of them were typically the tallest in the group unless they were with their cousins.

The rodeo crew kept the chaos that was mutton busting as contained as possible. Each time the gate opened, and a sheep bolted out with a little person attached to its back, the crowd erupted into cheers. Call it bias, but Vivienne swore the screams were louder when Daley shot out of the chute, gripping the sheep beneath him with his tight little arms and legs.

"That's it, Wake Up Call! Ride 'em, Boy!"

"Go, Dale!"

Rhine's voice mingled with the others cheering for Daley in the five and a half seconds he held on to the back of his mount without falling off. The time didn't seem very long.

But, seeing as some others fell off less than two seconds in, Daley's performance was outstanding.

Showing he was every bit his father's son, he stood up from the dirt without help, wiped his hands on his little protective vest, then threw one arm up as he followed the instructions of the rodeo helpers. Autumn caught Vivienne's eye, and the cousins shared a smile.

"Vivi, you've got a three-year-old man on your hands. What was that one arm in the air about?"

Shaking her head, Vivienne giggled.

"He was acknowledging the crowd. We were watching bull riding, and he saw some riders do that after they had a good ride. So now he does it."

"Lord... He is too much."

"Try living with him."

With a vigorous shake of her head, Autumn looked to where their daughters had their heads together.

"No, thank you. I have plenty to handle."

Vivienne leaving to escort Maya to the holding area cut their conversation short. The two met up with Daley and Vivienne's father, giving them the chance to congratulate Daley. Her son had insisted on his pop-pop being the one to be with him during competitions. Neither Vivienne nor Rhine argued the point. Her dad loved doing it, and it gave her and Rhine the chance to cheer for their son together.

As much as Maya was a daddy's girl, she only wanted Vivi with her for competition. Although it had been years since Vivienne had competed, the knowledge was still there. So, when the smile left her daughter's face and her expression shifted to extreme focus, Vivienne spoke to her softly, reminding her of the ways to get the most from Flower.

The moment before Maya was ready to mount her pony, Vivienne squeezed her shoulders, stooping until they were eye to eye.

"You're going to have an amazing ride, Maya. But I need you to do Mama a favor."

Cradling the side of her face, Vivienne smiled.

"Have fun."

Returning her smile, Maya nodded.

"Yes, ma'am."

Once Maya was in the saddle, Vivienne scrambled to the gate to get a good view of her baby girl in action. Seeing her daughter fly around the barrels filled her with pride and nostalgia. It didn't even matter if Maya had the best time. Vivienne wore a face-splitting grin as she watched her daughter enjoying herself doing something the two of them shared.

Later, everyone gathered at the Sunset, eating, laughing, and enjoying each other while they relived some events of the day and others from the past. As often happened when the family was together, Grandma Hattie held court. The matriarch had a wealth of stories to tell.

It was old news now, but she was reminding Rhine that he had her to thank for his happy family life.

"I told Clint and Pam, if they couldn't get my baby back down here where she belonged, I'd do it myself. It just so happened I did you a solid at the same time."

"And I will forever be in your debt, Granny."

Leaning over, Rhine kissed her cheek. Vivienne grinned at her grandmother swatting Rhine away while blushing.

"You go on now, Rhinehart Stephens. I was tired of seeing you wandering around Lone Star looking like a sick puppy. You and Vivi weren't fooling anyone other than yourselves. But you're welcome."

Pointing to her great-grandchildren running around with their cousins, her smile widened. She looked at Vivienne with a glint in her eyes. Coming to stand next to Rhine, Vivienne leaned into him as he wrapped an arm around her waist.

"I still can't believe you tricked me like that, Granny. Had me stressed out and running around trying to fix things, and all along you knew you never intended to sell this ranch."

"I did what needed to be done. Got you home, didn't it? Now you have a loving husband, beautiful children, and you run the best therapeutic horse ranch in the country."

Vivienne couldn't sustain her mock outrage in the face of her granny's praise. A blush heated her cheeks.

"Granny, I wouldn't say the best, but Sunset holds its own."

"I said what I said, Little Girl."

Rhine's hold tightened on Vivienne's waist, then he settled her in his lap.

"Don't argue with your elders, Rose. If Grandma Hattie says you're the best, then you're the best. I'm inclined to agree with her."

Placing a hand on Rhine's face, Vivienne lightly scratched his beard.

"You're biased."

"I'm not biased. I'm yours."

"Yes. Yes, you are...my Reluctant Cowboy."

The End

# *Let's Keep in Touch!*

Want to keep up with what's next and what's happening in my writing journey? Sign up for my monthly newsletter to get inside information, sneak peeks and excerpts!

https://sendfox.com/DarieMcCoy

Is the inside view from a newsletter not enough? To get more, you should join my Patreon. Tiers start as low as $5 per month. Depending on your subscription level, you'll receive many perks from reading along as I write, up to receiving customized book boxes.

# LET'S KEEP IN TOUCH!

https://patreon.com/DarieMcCoy

# Craving Her Cowboy

## SILVER CREEK RANCH BOOK 14

***They weren't looking for love. But some cravings are too dangerous to ignore.***

**Gavin McAllister** was born into power with a future carved out in politics. But Gavin chose combat boots over campaign trails, leaving behind his father's ambitions to serve in the Army. Now, scarred from years of war with a need to reconnect with who he truly is, Gavin's returned to the one place that ever offered him peace—Silver Creek Ranch, the secluded South Dakota sanctuary where wounded veterans go to heal.

He didn't come back looking for connection. And he sure as hell didn't come back looking for her.

**Asha Monroe** is a former Marine with a sharp mind and a guarded heart, she's fiercely independent—and struggling to adjust to a world that suddenly feels unfamiliar without the uniform. Silver Creek is supposed to be a brief pause, a place to reset. But Gavin? He's temptation wrapped in denim and silence. She sees the pain he tries to hide. He sees the fire she won't let anyone else touch.

When walls come down and desire takes hold, Gavin and Asha must face the truth: some battles are meant to be lost. And some hearts are worth the risk of breaking.

*Craving her Cowboy is the next book in the Silver Creek Ranch series. Grab your copy of Craving her Cowboy today!*

# Acknowledgments

First, thank you to Peyton Banks for allowing me to write again in the the wonderful Silver Creek Ranch world. I learned so much writing Rhine and Vivienne and I sincerely appreciate you welcoming me into the fold.

My sincere thanks to my Darlings, Delights, Decadents, and Divas. You ladies read my rough words, cheer me on, offer feedback to help me sharpen my pen. A special thanks to Michelle Jackson for lending me her military knowledge, answering my random questions to assist me in writing an authentic character.

As always, I thank my writing partners, Brianna Q. Price and Niccoyan Zheng. Without your support, I don't think I could have grown as an author as quickly as I have. There's still work to do, and I couldn't be happier to have you on this journey with me. Last but not least, thank you to all the readers and everyone who lends me guidance and support throughout this author journey. You're amazing. I don't have enough words to show my gratitude.

# About the Author

Darie McCoy is an independent author of contemporary, interracial, romantic suspense, and paranormal/shifter romance books. A reader first, she enjoys reading books across many genres although romance holds a special place in her heart. Her experience working in a STEM field offers her a unique perspective which she uses in each story she pens.

When she doesn't have her nose in a book or her fingers on the keyboard, Darie enjoys working in her vegetable garden. A serial hobbyist, she also enjoys knitting, sewing, baking and canning. One of her favorite treats to make is salted caramel popcorn. Amongst her friends, she's known to transport the sweet treat in large quantities to share whenever they get together.

Born and raised in the south, Darie stands by the staunchly held southern sentiments that the best tea is sweet tea and college football is life.

# Also by Darie McCoy

### Central Valley Pack Series
Chosen

Healed

Reclaimed

### Frost Family Series
For Real

Sano's Queen (A Novella)

Christmas Candy

### Draft Pick Series
Draft Pick Season I: Carver

Draft Pick Season II: Andrei

Draft Pick Season III: Denzel

Draft Pick Season IV: Vitaly (Patreon Exclusive)

### The Getaway Chronicles / The Blessings Series
The Glassmaker's Helper: The Getaway Chronicles

The Diviner's Soul

### The Protector Series
Ever

### Other books/stories
Involuntary

Just Kiss Me (Part of Cupid's Kiss Anthology)

Toad: Sin City MC Oakland

Controlled Desire: Fall of Desire

Construction Book Boyfriend (Book Boyfriend Series)

The Rancher's Home (Silver Creek Ranch Series)

**Darie McCoy writing as Midnight Locke**

Sexy Scenarios: Volume I

Teacher, TeacHer